27 x 9/11 LT 12/09

By the same author

The Great Psychedelic Armadillo Picnic

'Scuse Me While I Whip This Out

The Prisoner of Vandam Street

Curse of the Missing Puppethead

Kill Two Birds & Get Stoned

Guide to Texas Etiquette

Meanwhile Back at the Ranch

Steppin' on a Rainbow

The Mile High Club

Spanking Watson

Blast from the Past

Roadkill

The Love Song of J. Edgar Hoover

God Bless John Wayne

Armadillos & Old Lace

Elvis, Jesus & Coca-Cola

Musical Chairs

Frequent Flyer

When the Cat's Away

A Case of Lone Star

Greenwich Killing Time

TEN
LITTLE
NEW YORKERS

A NOVEL

Kinky Friedman

SIMON & SCHUSTER

New York • London • Toronto • Sydney

SIMON & SCHUSTER
Rockefeller Center
1230 Avenue of the Americas
New York, NY 10020

This book is a work of fiction. Names, characters,
places, and incidents either are products of the
author's imagination or are used fictitiously. Any
resemblance to actual events or locales or persons,
living or dead, is entirely coincidental.

SIMON & SCHUSTER and colophon are registered trademarks
of Simon & Schuster, Inc.

For information about special discounts for bulk purchases,
please contact Simon & Schuster Special Sales at
1-800-456-6798 or business@simonandschuster.com

Book design by Ellen R. Sasahara

Manufactured in the United States of America

3 5 7 9 10 8 6 4 2

Library of Congress Cataloging-in-Publication Data
Friedman, Kinky.
Ten little New Yorkers : a novel / Kinky Friedman.
p. cm.
1. New York (N.Y.)—Fiction. I. Title.

PS3556.R527T45 2005
813'.54—dc22   2004059158
ISBN 0-7432-4603-9

TEN
LITTLE
NEW YORKERS

PROLOGUE

Dear Reader,

This may not make much sense to you. I'm still in kind of a state of shock myself. So I'll let Kinky tell the story in his own words. I went over to his place on Vandam Street, you see, a few days after the tragedy. In the bottom lefthand drawer of his old desk, I found the notes he'd written concerning his last adventure, which comprise the manuscript you are about to read. I have not changed or edited the story in any way.

I'll tell you something else. That loft of Kinky's seemed so sad and lonely it broke my heart. The memories were as thick as the dust. I took the manuscript, scooped up the puppethead, then cleaned out the refrigerator. Didn't want anything to spoil. Then I said a little prayer for Kinky's soul and I got the hell out of there.

The Kinkster was more than just my best friend. I believe he was, as he often claimed, a true mender of destinies. It's just too bad there was no one around with the ability to help him mend his own. As for me, I will never forget him. For as long as I live, Kinky will be alive as well. I hope our little adventures will be read for many years to come. They were odd, at times quirky, and some of them were

1

resolved in quite unconventional ways, but all of them were fun, enlightening, colorful, and hopelessly human. And we lived them all together.

He was a great friend. He was a great detective. In fact, if Sherlock Holmes had come from Texas, his name would be Kinky Friedman.

Larry "Ratso" Sloman
New York, New York

ONE

The cat had been gone and the lesbian dance had been silent for some time now. It had been a fairly rough patch for the Kinkster. Ratso was really starting to irritate me as well. "Starting," I suppose, would be the wrong word to use. Ratso had been doing a pretty thorough job of getting up my sleeve ever since the first day I'd met him. Maybe it was part of his charm. Maybe I never used to let it get to me. Maybe with the cat gone and no one around to really talk to, the full brunt of Ratso's personality was finally weighing down upon me. But Ratso was a guy you just couldn't hate, so you might as well love him. And when I think of all the shit the two of us have been through together, I see him as a natural and inevitable part of my own existence. The cat never liked him, of course, and that would be putting it mildly. The truth was the cat fucking hated him, and I believe you should never mistrust the instincts of a cat. But what the hell, the cat by now was no doubt safely across the rainbow bridge and I was standing at my window, waiting for Ratso, and watching the rain.

It was a hard rain, as Bob Dylan might say, but I didn't mind. In fact, I didn't really give a damn if the whole city floated away. Well, maybe it'd be nice to keep Chinatown. When it's raining cats and dogs I miss the animals and people I've loved in my life and I feel closer to them and farther away from today. Today is just a garbage-man in his yellow raincoat. Today is the wet woman with the wild hair walking willfully into the white wall. Today's a goddamn vase without any flowers. Hell, give me a passably decent tomorrow, I said. Give me a handful of scrappy yesterdays. Give me liberty or give me death or give me life on the Mississippi.

Since my cat had disappeared I found I was talking to myself a great deal, and myself, unfortunately, had never taken the time or effort to bother developing her listening skills. Without the cat I was a starfish on the sand. A lesbian dance class without the music. A Japanese tourist wandering the world without a camera. I was lost in a swirling gray fog of grief and self-pity. What the hell, I thought. Being alone provides an opportunity few of us ever have in life, the opportunity to get to know ourselves. I mean you might as well get to know yourself. You're going to have to live together.

I watched the rain some more. It felt like it was raining all over the world. Everywhere but Georgia. I heard some rumbling sounds from upstairs. Lesbian thunder no doubt. Then from further upstairs I heard the rumbling sounds of just plain thunder. After listening for a while it was hard to tell which was which. Ask me if I cared. Large dogs often seem to be afraid of thunder, but small dogs usually remain unfazed by it. What does this tell us? Not too much. These are the kinds of fragmented thoughts that quite commonly pop into the heads of private investigators who've gone too long with nothing to investigate. If this situation persists for a while, said investigators may even lose their powers of observation. When this occurs, about all they can do is watch the rain.

"If I'm not mistaken," I said to the cat who wasn't there, "I hear the call of a blue-buttocked tropical loon."

It is not uncommon, psychologists say, for a person to speak to a loved one after the loved one has passed away. The force of habit is often stronger than the force of gravity. The force of wishful thinking, I would submit, may even be stronger than the other two. Psychologists probably wouldn't agree with me. Like that red-bearded baboon who got me deselected from the Peace Corps. Because I was honest with him I never got to meet a blonde driving a jeep in Africa and make her the future ex–Mrs. Kinky Friedman. I had to wander the country aimlessly for many moons, retrain in Hawaii, then go to Borneo where I helped people who'd been farming successfully for over two thousand years. It was during my stint in Borneo that my penis sloughed off in the jungle. I didn't blame God. I didn't blame the psychologist. I didn't even blame the naked little brown children who laughed and pointed to my penis lying there on the jungle floor and shouted *Pisang! Pisang* means "banana" in Malay. No, I don't blame any of these people. I just blame my editor for leaving this shit out of the book.

The blue-buttocked tropical loon called out again, giving forth with what sounded like another, somewhat more impassioned, mating call. What, I wondered, was a blue-buttocked tropical loon doing in the middle of a rainstorm in the West Village? The blue-buttocked tropical loon belonged in a rain forest, not a rainstorm. Of course I could understand it making an occasional appearance in the East Village, but it was highly unusual for this rare bird to migrate to the more civilized West Village. Another unsettling irregularity was that it was the middle of winter, certainly not the normal mating season for the blue-buttocked tropical loon. Possibly, like everybody else in the world, the loon was merely out to fuck me. I opened the kitchen window ever so slightly. I looked down into a monolithic gray wall of rain but could see nothing. Then I heard the strange sound again.

"Kinkstah!" it seemed to say. "Kinkstah, I'm fucking drowning out here!"

I walked over to the roaring fireplace and picked up the little black puppethead from off the mantel. The key to the building was still wedged firmly in its smiling mouth. It seemed it was the only secure thing I had in the world these days. The puppethead had been lost, but now it was found, and it held the key, I felt, to my last remaining chance for happiness in life. If you're happy, of course, this probably won't make much sense to you. If you're not, you probably already realize how the world turns on a dime. Or a key. Or a memory.

I opened the window a little further and threw poor Yorick out into the cold curtain of rain. Somewhere below that curtain stood either Ratso or an extremely articulate blue-buttocked tropical loon. Moments later all doubt was erased as Ratso came stumbling into the loft like a carnival tent coming in from the rain. He was wearing a fire-engine-red hooded rain slicker that flapped and dripped all the way to the refrigerator.

"My floors will be a mess," I said.

"Your floors have always been a mess," said Ratso. "Why change now? At least you've gotten rid of all those cat turds—"

Realizing his own unpremeditated insensitivity, perhaps, he pulled his head out of the refrigerator long enough to walk the puppethead back to its customary perch on top of the mantel. Then, with one arm resting on the mantel, he warmed himself before the fire.

"Sorry," he said.

"Forget it," I told him. And I meant it. The loss of one cat, one man, one woman, one child, one dream, signifies very little either in the city or in the world. Everybody knows there's plenty more where that one came from. Nobody cares or everybody does—it's all the same thing. We mourn for ourselves, I thought. So get on with your life or become a fucking Buddhist or something, but don't just sit around moping about it. Simply make a point in the future of never letting yourself get involved with anything that eats or dies.

"Cheer up, Kinkstah!" said Ratso. "Let's go to Chinatown."

"That would constitute eating."

"Eating's important, Kinkstah! So's dumping. When you stop eating, you stop dumping. When you stop dumping, you stop living. The Jewish people have been assuaging their grief and their guilt for over two thousand years—hell, maybe more—by eating Chinese food. Why stop now? We have a great tradition to uphold!"

"Ratso, it's raining."

"That's what they told Noah! And what'd he do? He built himself an ark!"

"Maybe I'll build myself something like this," I said.

With impeccable timing, I blasted a loud fart that seemed to reverberate in the loft, echoing like footsteps in the tomb of the mummy of the Pharaoh Esophagus. Ratso was impressed.

"That was a bell-ringer," he said. "Did you touch cloth?"

"That would be unlikely, Watson. As you well know, I've worn no underwear since my years in the tropics. I prefer to go commando-style."

"Right you are, Sherlock. How could I forget a thing like that?"

"Ah, my dear Watson! But it is exactly the trivial little matter like that that the criminal mind often forgets. And it is exactly 'a thing like that,' as you say, that arouses the rational, scientific mind of the detective and leads him to the sure resolution of the most puzzling and convoluted matter."

"That's brilliant, Sherlock. But there are also health ramifications to not wearing underwear. Your pee-pee could catch a cold."

"Ah, Watson! How I have missed your witty banter and camaraderie by the fireside! You never fail to bring a delightful, if somewhat earthy, humor to an investigation."

"We have an investigation?"

"Alas, Watson, the answer is no."

"When *will* we have an investigation, Sherlock?"

"We'll never have one if you keep going around in that ridiculous Little Red Riding Hood outfit. But don't you fear, Watson. Investigations are like cats. They are fated to come into and go out of our lives. One way or another, they will come around again."

TWO

To lose a cat in a big city is one of the greatest tragedies God can throw at you. Some, who've been spiritually deprived since childhood, don't have a clue what it means to have a cat, lose a cat, love a cat, or be a cat. When a child is lost or runs away, or a spouse goes out for cigarettes and never comes back, part of the sadness comes with the realization, heavily laced with guilt, that they don't want to return. Even if the cat, man, woman, child is a total asshole, you always tend to blame yourself. Maybe if I'd only cut his little grapefruit up in neat segments the way he liked, he wouldn't have left me. Maybe if I'd been stronger, maybe if I'd been gentler, maybe if I'd been green or black or blue or whatever it is that I'm not and could never be, then this shit wouldn't have happened. People of good conscience always tend to blame themselves but the truth is that the fucking cat just wanted to see the world. Or the lover got tired of you or didn't like the way you ate bagels or thought he was king of the gypsies. He or she was very much like the cat. They all wanted out.

But when a human wants to come back, all he has to do is come back. Even a small child can tell somebody, "I want to go home." A cat can never do this, even if it wants to. The cat must depend upon the humanity of a cold world. Of course, I suppose there are times when so must we all.

Ratso finally succeeded in his efforts to suck, fuck, or cajole me out of the loft. The rain, I noticed, had abated somewhat. It was no longer a biblical downpour. Now it was merely a fine mist with an occasional teardrop ladled in to keep it honest. Ratso and I decided it might be bracing to walk to Chinatown, so we ankled it up Vandam and across to SoHo. As fate would have it, we passed a building on Prince Street with a cat watching us carefully from a large bay window. Possibly the cat's interest was piqued by Ratso's bright-red hooded outfit.

"You know," I said, "whenever I used to see a cat in a window before, I used to say to myself, 'I have my cat and that's somebody else's cat.'"

"That's a brilliant fucking observation, Sherlock."

"Now that my cat is gone, I don't say that anymore. Now I say, 'Every cat is my cat.' Especially the strays."

"Cuddles was a stray," said Ratso. "I still remember the night we found her."

I remembered it, too. It was so cold Jesus was pissing icicles. We found Cuddles in a shoebox in an alley off Mott Street. The U.S. Olympic hockey team had just beaten the Russians. Ratso had been ecstatic. I'd been moderately pleased myself. Cuddles had merely been cold. Of course, her name wasn't Cuddles yet. She was just a tiny black-and-white kitten, all alone, freezing to death in a shoebox in Chinatown. We named her Cuddles after Kacey Cohen. It'd been her nickname in school. I picked up the little kitten and put her in the warm pocket of my coat and took her home. I wished I could've done the same for Kacey, but it was too late for that.

"I just hope heaven looks like Chinatown in the rain," I said.

A soft comforting pillow of raindrops had started to fall past the neon walls of Mott Street as Ratso and I marched determinedly onward into the oblivious night. When we came to 67 Mott Street, we ankled a sharp right into Big Wong's. Just before we entered the establishment, however, we both partook of a little tradition that had grown up between us over the years. We stood out on the sidewalk like two Depression-era shivering souls watching the friendly Chinese cooks ladling noodles into the huge steaming pots of soup. The cooks, indeed, were so familiar with Ratso and myself that they would occasionally dash a ladle of soup against the window to playfully startle us out of our mesmerized state. This, it seemed, was a very big joke to them. Ratso and I, I now believe, very possibly knew something they didn't. We knew that life was the joke.

"Don't be so hard on yourself," said Ratso, as the waiter showed us to our customary table right next to the stairs that led down to the dumper. Was it possible, I wondered, that for the first time all day, Ratso had noticed my fragile, world-weary demeanor? Maybe I *was* being too hard on myself. Hell, I'd already tried blaming everybody else for the apparent shipwreck that was my life. My sister Marcie had told me an old Vietnamese saying that very possibly applied here. "Whenever you point the finger of blame at somebody else, just remember there are three fingers pointing back at you."

"The truth is," Ratso was saying, "that no amateur private investigator in the city has solved as many high-profile cases as you, Sherlock. It's a little boring for both of us when you don't have a case. That's because neither of us has a day job. Or a life, for that matter."

"If those are intended as words of comfort, Watson," I said, "your bedside manner may require a trip to the cleaners."

"What would you rather hear, Sherlock? Some bullshit bedside manner, or the truth? The truth is you're the greatest detective in New York and you don't even seem to know it. You've cracked cases that the NYPD and the FBI only wished they could've solved. You're just coming off one of your biggest years and you're singin' the blues.

Okay, so your cat ran away—"

"The cat did not run away."

"Okay. The cat booked reservations on the *QE2* and took a sabbatical to the south of France. What's the difference? The cat's gone but you're still here, and you've got some pretty impressive notches on your cigar this year. You found the missing puppethead, or rather, the cat found it. What the hell?"

"The cat *did* find the puppethead," I said thoughtfully. "Maybe there *is* something to the *Curse of the Missing Puppethead*."

"I can't believe a great scientific mind like yours is telling me this shit. Sherlock, get a grip on yourself! Fuck the puppethead! You found the hit-and-run killer of Big Jim Cravotta's kid! You saved Chinga's life! Aren't you proud of that?"

"I don't know. He doesn't call. He doesn't write."

Somewhere in the course of this inquisition Ratso managed to order about seven dishes for the two of us. I had hoped that once the food arrived it might occupy his attention for a while, but sadly, that was not to be the case. He just continued to talk and eat at the same time, and it was not a pleasant spectacle to observe.

"What about *The Prisoner of Vandam Street*, Kinkstah? Yeah. *The Prisoner of Vandam Street*. Remember? You were right and everybody else was wrong! Remember that one, Kinkstah?"

"Can't say I do, Watson, it's happened so often. That's how I know I'm right. When everybody else is wrong."

"So that's your secret."

"You see, Watson, this is why I never reveal my methods. Once I explain it, some asshole, present company excluded, of course, always thinks it's easy. It's really not that important whether you're right or wrong, it's what you do with it. Willie Nelson, whom I call 'the Hillbilly Dalai Lama,' always says: 'Keep doin' it wrong 'til you like it that way.'"

"But can't you at least enjoy all your successes, Sherlock?"

"Of course not. A mender of destinies never enjoys his successes, Watson. Ask Rambam."

"*You* ask Rambam."

"I have. He hates it when he puts somebody in prison. The same with Kent Perkins. I once asked him where he was going and he said, 'To Arizona, to ruin a man's life.' People I've helped put away hate me. They'd kill me if they could. Their families hate me. Their children hate me. The cops hate me. Our waiter hates me. Everybody hates me, Watson."

"That's because you're a sick fuck, Sherlock."

"Ah, Watson, how very intuitive you are! Indeed I am a sick fuck, as you say. I am sick of what you call my successes. Yet only one thing can make me well."

"What's that, Sherlock?"

"Justice, Watson. Justice."

"Have you tried the roast pork over scrambled eggs," he said.

THREE

I'm not sure Ratso ever understood the weight that rests upon the spiritual shoulders of the mender. I also don't know how well Theo really understood Vincent. He loved him, of course. He was the only one who ever bought a fucking painting. The other artists loved the sunshine, it was said, but Van Gogh loved the sun. When you die, he said, you just take a train to a star. It's hard to understand a guy like that. You can't blame Theo or Ratso or Paul or John or Luke. It's sometimes enough just to know when you're in the presence of greatness. The great man himself may be a total clueless asshole, but maybe that's part of what makes him great. He doesn't just sing the song—his magic is that he gives it to you.

What I'm saying is that Ratso, in a fine Dr. Watson–like manner, skipped blithely through our little adventures, never fully realizing that each one took away another little piece of Janis's heart. Like the other Village Irregulars, he felt the excitement of the hunt. Like the others, he felt the joy of being a part of something bigger than himself. But in the end, he didn't feel the weight, and he didn't feel the hate. None of them did. Except Rambam, of course. He was a licensed private investigator. He understood what it was like to stand in a dark alley somewhere, trying not to play God. But there weren't any support groups for this kind of thing. You just did it as long as you could. Then you packed your busted valise and took a train to a star.

It was a particularly cold winter in New York. It always seemed to be particularly cold in New York. Maybe it was because I was usually in Texas in the summertime. Like a bird of passage, I would drift down there to thaw out, dry out, and generally hobnob with all the friendly ghosts of Echo Hill. Echo Hill invariably made me feel rich in the coin of the spirit. Then I'd head back up to New York and freeze my assets. To paraphrase Dr. Jim Bone, I found myself living between the legend and the lamppost. I didn't have a home. I didn't want a home. For way too long now I'd been homesick for heaven.

I sat down at my old battle-scarred desk, hoisted the cap from Holmes's cranium, and reached deep inside his brains for a Cuban cigar. I took my trusty butt-cutter out of my pocket and lopped off another butt. Some measure their lives by when their passports expire. Some measure their lives in coffee spoons. Some measure their lives in butts, Cuban cigar or otherwise. I belonged to the latter butt-measuring category. I fired up the cigar just about the time the phones started ringing.

As you might or might not be aware, I have two red telephones at opposite ends of my desk, and they've been there so long I'm not even sure anymore *why* they're there. I'm not even sure anymore why *I'm* here. Maybe the red telephones represent the whorehouse of the human spirit. Maybe my presence indicates the return of the whore. Maybe you know the answers better than I do. Maybe you should be writing the fucking book and I should be over there in the rocking chair by the fire saying, "What's this asshole nattering on about?"

I picked up the blower on the left. I puffed pontifically on the cigar for a brief moment.

"Start talkin'," I said.

"Dis is Big Jim Cravotta and I'm comin' over dere ta rip your heart out!"

"You're too late."

"Jesus Christ," said Rambam. "Are you still feeling fucking sorry for yourself?"

"Who better to feel sorry for?"

"How about me? My Jewish dominatrix turned out to be a born-again lesbian working for the ATF."

"That's a shame."

"Not really. I'd rather be the spanker than the spankee."

I leaned back in the chair and puffed patriotically on the cigar as a small parade passed before my eyes of all the crazy shit Rambam and I had done together on both sides of the law. I saw the American flag going by. Then the flag of Israel. Then the Texas flag.

"I said, 'I'd rather be the spanker than the spankee,'" said Rambam.

"Is there an echo in this room?"

"Is there an echo in this room?"

I puffed the cigar for a long moment and watched the smoke of life drift upward to the man-made sky.

"What the hell's wrong with you, Kinky? I know you very fucking well, but I've never known you to be this blue this long. I've seen your smiles, your frowns, your ups, your downs. I can't really say that I've ever grown accustomed to your face. But I've got to tell you, you do sound pretty fucked up."

"It's been a rough year."

"Everybody's had a rough year. Why is this little private investigator different from all other little private investigators?"

"I miss my cat."

"I miss my Jewish dominatrix. Hold on. I'm going to stitch that one onto my holster. That is, after I blow a few holes in the ceiling to shut up these neighbors."

"Try living under a lesbian dance class."

"You call that living?"

"Not really."

Things had been so quiet lately that even Winnie Katz's little Isle of Lesbos had not seemed to be making its presence known to man. The loft felt emptier without the cat and the lesbians. The whole city felt hollow.

"Look, man," said Rambam, "if things are really that bad, maybe you ought to get out of here for a while. You could go to Hawaii and hang out with your friend Hoover."

"Hoover's busy writing features for the *Honolulu Advertiser* about saving the descendants of Princess Kaiulani's flock of peacocks from being euthanized by some condominium committee."

"Why don't they just euthanize the condominium committee?"

"Hoover suggested that, I believe. When Princess Kaiulani died at the age of twenty-three, the royal peacocks all cried, as did the people of Hawaii. Now they have Starbucks and the Hula Bowl and the fucking condominium committee. To paraphrase Bob Dylan, now is the time for their tears."

"Why don't you go back to Texas for a while? Help Cousin Nancy and Tony with the Rescue Ranch. Working at Utopia might be just what the doctor ordered."

"I can't work at Utopia. I'm the Gandhi-like figure. Gandhi-like figures never work."

"Tell me about it. I'm watching about seventeen of them right now in the street outside my window. They're all watching one guy with a shovel. Of course they don't call themselves Gandhi-like figures. They call themselves City of New York maintenance workers."

I could see the whole picture in my mind. Rambam standing at his window watching the seventeen maintenance workers standing around on the street watching the one guy working with the shovel. Most of us, I reflected, are just like them. We are merely observers of life. We leave the real digging and the heavy lifting to others. Why get your hands dirty if you don't have to?

"You could go to Vegas," Rambam was saying. "You always liked Vegas."

"What are you? A fucking travel agent?"

"Go visit your magician friends, Penn and Teller. Maybe they can make your grumpy attitude disappear."

This, I felt, was truly the pot calling the kettle black. Rambam had enormous grumpy potential himself. It was just that whenever one of us became deeply depressed, the other one would become positively chirpy. This, of course, proved all the more irritating to the one who was grumpy.

"What was that your dad always used to say about being depressed?"

"Oh, yeah. 'Cheer up. It only gets worse.'"

"He was right, by the way. But don't let it bother you. If you refuse to leave the city, your only alternative is to stay busy."

"I know that, Dr. Freud. The problem is, like the great Sherlock Holmes, I'm currently between cases."

"You are aware," said Rambam, "that Sherlock Holmes was a fictional character."

"Scientists aren't sure of this."

"Jesus Christ!"

"They're not sure of him either."

I liked people who may or may not have existed. People like King Arthur and Robin Hood and myself. Maybe the great detective of Baker Street wasn't real. Maybe he was merely the thinking man's Jesus Christ. Maybe if Jesus were around today he'd be doing what I was doing. Maybe he'd be standing around Times Square listening to people telling him to get a job. Maybe he'd get a job. Maybe his job would be standing around outside Rambam's window with all his disciples watching a guy with a shovel. Maybe not.

"Kinky? Are you there?"

"Part of me's here. Part of me's wandering around some alley in the dark."

"That's okay, I guess. Just as long as nobody ties tin cans to your tail."

FOUR

According to my friend, Dylan Ferrero, guys our age are in the seventh-inning stretch. I'm well aware that this rather arcane sports analogy may be lost upon Iranian mullahs and non–baseball fans, so let's just say that most of the game is over. Perhaps everybody does know what the seventh-inning stretch implies, it's just that most of the world is too young or too busy to take the time to care about what it means to baseball or to life. A lot of important and wonderful things can happen, of course, after the seventh-inning stretch, but statistically speaking, it's pretty fucking late in the game.

More evidence of just how late it was could probably be elucidated from knowing that Dylan Ferrero pulled a muscle in his back recently while wiping his ass. This may seem a moderately repellent tidbit of information, but it's true. None of us are getting any younger and none of us are getting any smarter. About all we can hope for is wise or lucky. We're old enough to realize and young enough to know that when the Lord closes the door, he opens a little window.

Still, I missed the cat. And I missed the trials and the tribulations and the joys and the sorrows of Yesterday Street. And I even missed Winnie Katz and the lesbian dance class. As irritating and unpleasant as the peripatetic pounding on the ceiling had always seemed in the past, now that the whole place was silent I somehow missed it. What the hell, I thought, even lesbians need to take a vacation sometimes. Maybe the Kinkster needed one as well. Except it's kind of hard to go on a vacation when your whole life's already a vacation. Everybody goes on a vacation from something. You can't really go on a vacation from nothing, can you? But this was the very thing that Ratso could never understand. A mender of destinies cannot conjure up cases and adventures and damsels in distress and investigations of sordid natures out of the whole cloth of life as we know it. Even a mender of destinies must await his destiny. And mine, in this high-tech, jet-set world, appeared to be arriving by Pony Express.

Anyway, it wasn't my job to fulfill Ratso's fantasies about being Dr. Watson with the game afoot. If he wanted a game he could turn on his television set. All the Irregulars in the world couldn't be of any use if you didn't have a case. And I didn't have a case. I didn't even have a cat. All I really had was a great urge to kill myself by jumping through a ceiling fan. But I didn't have a ceiling fan.

So here I was in the seventh-inning stretch, no cat, no case, no ceiling fan, trying to decide where to go for my fucking vacation. What the hell, I thought. Maybe I'd just take Jim Morrison's advice: "The West is the best." He died, of course, in a bathtub in Paris. He had a dog named Sage, however. Sage grows in the West. In New York nothing grows, unless you want to count a rotating crop of tedious. So in the West you had Texas, Vegas, and Hawaii. They were all magical places but they were so far away. Yet as the gypsy said, "From where?"

And as I kicked around ideas for my supposed vacation, an evil festered in the city, an evil the likes of which I had not encountered in many years. It pulsed through the heart and coursed through the veins of the gray familiar architecture that was New York. It was not a case yet. It was not an investigation yet. It was not murder. Yet.

It was not my nature to imbue myself with a prescience I did not possess. For no man, no matter how intuitive or how wise, could see the future. All I can tell you is that I felt this nameless, faceless evil in my bones. As it formed in the mind of another, I could feel it quiver in my soul.

FIVE

Things do seem a little dead tonight," said McGovern from the barstool on my left at the Monkey's Paw.

"Dead?" I said. "This town was dead before the virus hit."

"New York's a bit like Vegas. It never really sleeps. It just nods out every once in a while."

"Is that why we're the only two people in the bar?"

McGovern looked around at the drab, seedy ambience of the Monkey's Paw. The sheer emptiness of the place was stunning.

"Do you think we should take this personally?" he asked.

"Hell no," I said. "I never take anything personally."

"That's not what I hear," said McGovern. "I hear you're miserable and you're blaming everybody but yourself."

"Who told you that?" I said. "Mother Teresa?"

"She's dead."

"You're kidding. Maybe she died of ennui on a visit to New York."

"I don't know why you're whining about New York, Kink. This old town has been fucking great to you. You came up here from Texas like some cowboy off a trail ride and the whole place has embraced you like one of its own. In fact, it's done a hell of a lot more than that. This city's made you a fucking hero."

I signaled Tommy the bartender for another pint of Guinness. I watched McGovern drain his tall Vodka McGovern and motion to Tommy as well. I didn't feel like a fucking hero. I felt, to paraphrase Adlai Stevenson when he lost to Eisenhower, like a little kid who'd stubbed his toe in the dark. I felt too big to cry, but it hurt too much to laugh.

"I mean it, Kink," McGovern was yammering on. "You've gotten more ink recently than a goddamn giant squid. There was a time when I was the Lone Ranger, the only guy in town who was bothering to chronicle your successes. Now the media's all over you. Every time you solve a case they just about have a ticker-tape parade for you. You're the Sherlock Holmes of Manhattan! Millions of people read about your exploits! They love to see you catch the criminals that elude the cops. And don't forget, Sherlock Holmes was only a fictional character. You're a real human being."

It was a long speech for McGovern, and, indeed, it was an impassioned one. It was so impassioned in fact that his fresh Vodka McGovern stood virtually untouched on the mahogany, an occurrence that I'd only seen happen once before many years ago when McGovern's attention had been entirely focused upon the sirenlike embrace of a certain auburn-haired woman. The exhortation itself carried echoes of Ratso's pep talk to me earlier in the day. Both were extremely well intentioned, if somewhat misguided. Both had the unfortunate effect of falling upon deaf ears. Both were rather poignant in their way, like the words of a child attempting to lift the spirit of an adult friend. Yet McGovern had managed to place his large Irish finger on what I'm sorry to say was precisely the problem. I was not a fictional character. I was a human being. And I was getting tired of this shit.

"All of these exploits, as you call them," I said, as McGovern took a deep, deserved drink of his Vodka McGovern, "might finally make a thick scrapbook some day, if anybody in this modern age still keeps scrapbooks. That's all our adventures have been good for, McGovern. A fucking scrapbook. And you know what happens to all scrapbooks sooner or later? Cats piss on them. Jesus, I miss the cat."

McGovern took another drink from his tall glass. He was a tall man, I thought darkly, let him drink from a tall glass. He could drink from the fucking Holy Grail for all I cared. If he wanted to end his days drinking at the Monkey's Paw, so be it. As for me, it was half-past time for my body and soul to find a healthier environment. Some place like Texas where people still believed in Santa Claus and many of them looked like Santa Claus and crime was not so subtle and fiendishly convoluted and mentally taxing upon the investigator. On the other hand, crime down there was possibly even more violent. Like that lady in Houston who gave her kids a Texas bath.

"It's not just the cat that you miss, although I know you two were very close. I think right now you're missing the excitement of the hunt. There haven't really been any challenging investigations lately for you to practice your deductive reasoning or whatever you like to call it. Three men were murdered in the Village this week, but their deaths were apparently unrelated so I doubt if you'd care to get involved."

"Each man's death diminishes me, McGovern," I said. "But you're essentially correct. They may diminish me, but they just don't interest me. It's kind of sad really."

"So it is," said McGovern.

We drank a few more rounds, but there was no joy in it. As we left the place and walked into the night to go our separate ways, I was struck once again by the intelligence and the humanity in McGovern's eyes. They were like a dog's eyes. You can always spot intelligence and humanity in a dog's eyes easier than you can in the eyes of a human being. There it was again. I couldn't get away from it. I was a human being.

As I legged it over to Vandam Street and McGovern wandered off to God knows where, I felt the sadness one feels when parting from the company of a true friend. He didn't know it yet, I thought, but we probably wouldn't be seeing each other again for a very long time.

SIX

That night I dreamed of my dearly departed parents, of campfire embers burning bright, of green hills, of shady canyons, of sparkling rivers running in the summer sun. My heart had traveled as far away from the city as it could get and I'd always believed you should follow your heart. I took the dream as a sign—a sign that pointed to Texas.

In the morning I knew what I had to do, which wasn't much. I made some espresso, fired up my first cigar of the morning, and booked a flight that night to Texas, which cost about nine million dollars but was a bargain at twice the price. Simon and Garfunkel were right about New York City winters bleeding you. Ratso, Rambam, and McGovern had been right, too. Get out while I still could, while the gettin' was good, while I still had a shard of a reputation left as a successful private investigator. Get out before the golden door hit me on the ass.

Would I ever return? I wondered, as I sat at my lonely desk, sipping the hot, bitter espresso. That remained to be seen. I walked my cigar and espresso over to the kitchen window and gazed down fondly at Vandam Street. In spite of it all, I would miss this place. For many months I'd stood at this very window and watched for a sign of the cat. Now I no longer believed I'd see her again. She was a lost love now. She was part of me and part of the brick and mortar of New York. Part of the morning and garbage cans and nights and light rain. Part of where I'd come from and part of where I was going.

Since I had no idea how long I'd be gone, and I could no longer leave the cat in charge, I figured I'd call Winnie Katz and ask her to kind of keep an eye on the place. In the past, I'd left the cat and the key to the loft with her whenever I'd left town. She'd proved herself to be fairly responsible, in spite of my private belief that she was trying to spiritually indoctrinate the cat into the wonderful world of lesbianism. Well, it didn't matter now. If Winnie'd drop the mail on my desk once in a while and make sure that teenage satanic cults weren't conducting rituals in the loft during my absence, I felt sure that Sherlock and Yorick could get by on their own for a while. At least they wouldn't be lonely. Two heads are better than one.

I called Winnie and she agreed, I thought somewhat grudgingly, to allow me to ascend to her Sapphic retreat to drop off the key. What had happened to people these days, I wondered? Whatever became of being a good neighbor? All I was doing was dropping off a fucking key. How hard was it to occasionally keep an eye on an empty loft? Hell, I'd been doing that for years.

But maybe there was another explanation for Winnie's seeming lack of graciousness. Perhaps things were going as slowly for her as they were for me. Maybe McGovern was right—the city was taking a little power nap, and its denizens would just have to deal with it. If you were a single person with an unconventional lifestyle, no family, no regular work, you just felt it more than others who probably welcomed a break from the rat race. That was all it was, I figured. If Winnie had had a Texas to go to, she probably would've gone there. Unfortunately, if you lived in New York long enough, you began to believe there was nowhere else to go.

It was about three espressos and two cigars later that I trudged stolidly up the stairs to Winnie's loft. It didn't really bother me that my last act, before packing and leaving town, was to give my key to a lesbian. If the truth be told, I was starting to like lesbians a bit in my twilight years. They didn't like me much, of course, but you can't have everything. I knocked assertively upon Winnie's door.

There was no answer. I knocked louder, identifying myself. Was there a precise etiquette for visiting a lesbian? I pounded on the door. At last, there came a shout from inside the loft. Moments later, I heard a chain being removed. Then another. Then another. Just a typical New Yorker preparing to greet a caller.

"Hang on, cowboy!" she shouted. "The stage ain't leavin' yet!"

Finally the knob turned and the door swung open to reveal a radiant Winnie Katz wrapped almost entirely in a red-and-blue Navajo rug. Her eyes shined. Her hair shined. Her face shined. There was just something about her you, perhaps quite literally, couldn't put your finger on. If I hadn't known she was a lesbian, I would have said that she was pregnant.

"You look great," I said. "Nice rug."

"Navajo rug," she said. "It's a song by Jerry Jeff Walker, as you probably know. Written by Ian Tyson."

"I didn't know you were a music lover."

"I'm a discerning music lover," she said, looking at me rather dismissively. "Where's the key, cowboy?"

I handed her the key. She started to tuck it into her bra, and then realized that it wasn't there.

"I mean it, Winnie," I said. "You look absolutely terrific. What's your secret?"

"My secret is I told all the girls in the dance class to take five."

"As in five minutes?"

"As in five months. Now I can do what I want to do. What about you, you big private dick? Why are you leaving town this time?"

"Like yourself, I'm doing what I want to do. I'm going back to Texas for a while. I told Ratso and the other Village Irregulars to keep a lid on crime until I get back."

"Ratso is a disgusting worm," said Winnie, pulling her Navajo rug more tightly around her body. "He disrupted my dance classes for about four months trying to get into everybody's leotards. Finally I threw him out."

"You were only with him for four months. I've been with him for twenty-five years."

"Why do you do it?"

"I took pity on him. I figure any heterosexual man who gets tossed out of a lesbian dance class, I mean, where's he going to go from there?"

Winnie smirked. Then she lit a Pall Mall. Then she smiled, waved, and closed the door. I stood in the hallway thinking back to when relations between Winnie and myself were bordering on sexual. Like any normal heterosexual man, I deluded myself with the notion that I could turn Winnie and make her forgo the lesbian faith. Like any fool, I tried and failed. Like any lesbian, she hated men all the more for their infernal meddling with her sexuality. Like any man, I was left wondering in dark hallways about the details of lesbian honeymoons.

Three hours later I was in a Checker cab flying through the cold concrete canyons of the city on my way to La Guardia. Outside my window it was dark and wet and miserable. Inside the cab I felt safe and warm and glad to be on my way to anywhere. I thought fleetingly of Ratso and Rambam and Winnie and McGovern and all the other characters I'd known over the years in New York. Though they most assuredly would continue to populate my heart, here they would stay forever.

I looked out the cab window, staring at block after block, building after building, brick after brick of desperate, dying architecture, inhabited almost incidentally by broken, bewildered souls, and I thought maybe I'm projecting, but right now I'd like to give it all back to the Indians because it wasn't worth the twenty-four dollars and it definitely wasn't worth the handful of colored beads.

SEVEN

The first things I did after arriving at the airport in Austin were to rent a four-wheeled penis, stock up on provisions, and head out to the ranch, deep in the heart of the Texas Hill Country. The Utopia Rescue Ranch, a never-kill sanctuary for animals run by Cousin Nancy Parker and her husband, Tony Simons, had recently moved from Utopia to our ranch, Echo Hill, just outside of Medina. The Rescue Ranch would still be called Utopia, we had decided, because it was. Now it resided on a beautiful fifty-acre flat that had formerly been the dump, which Cousin Nancy found highly humorous. I pointed out to her that when the great archaeologist Schliemann had discovered the famous, fabled, historic city of Troy, he'd had to dig through eleven levels of shit from ensuing generations. Cousin Nancy still found it amusing that her doublewide trailer now resided directly on top of what had previously been the Echo Hill dump. I tried to explain to her about the deep philosophical implications, but all she kept saying was, "The deeper, the better."

Now, under a full moon, I headed down the dusty country road to the ranch, as if under the inexorable power of that gentle magnet called home. Deer and jackrabbits gamboled and skittered by in the

35

moonlight and one solitary porcupine trundled slowly across the road like a little old man. The porcupine was clearly not in a hurry and, now that I thought about it, neither was I. I was merely a human reflection in this ageless, bucolic moonlight sonata.

When I pulled up in front of the lodge, the dogs all came out to greet me. Cousin Nancy and Tony had thoughtfully brought them over from the Rescue Ranch so I wouldn't have to spend my first night in Texas alone. It was a rather amazing adjustment to make. I had traded being surrounded by millions of oblivious, uncaring two-legged animals for being embraced by a small, loving family of four-legged animals. So far, it seemed like a pretty good deal.

I slept that night in the old lodge with a shotgun under my bed and a cat on my head. The cat's name was Lady Argyle and she used to belong to my mother before Min stepped on a rainbow. It is not a pleasant situation when you have a cat who insists upon sleeping on your head like a hat and all night long putting her whiskers in your nostril at intervals of about twenty-seven minutes. I haven't actually timed this behavioral pattern, but it wouldn't surprise me if the intervals were precisely twenty-seven minutes. This precarious set of affairs could have easily resulted in a hostage situation or a suicide pact but, fortunately, neither occurred. The two reasons are because I love Lady as much as a man is capable of loving a cat, and Lady loves me as much as a cat is capable of loving a man. It's not terribly surprising that the two of us were that close. After all, Cuddles was her mother.

It is a blessing when an independent spirit like a cat loves you, and it's a common human failing to underestimate or trivialize such a bond. On the other hand, it's not a healthy thing to observe a man going to bed with a cat on his head. And, in the case of Lady and myself, there *were* observers.

The observers of this Van Gogh mental hospital scenario were five dogs, all of whom despise Lady—though not half as much as Lady despises them. The dogs sleep on the bed, too, and they find it unnerving, not to say unpleasant, to be in the presence of a man who has a cat on his head. I've tried to discuss this with them on innumerable occasions, but it isn't easy to state your case to five dogs who are looking at you with pity in their eyes.

Mr. Magoo is eight years old and highly skilled at how to be resigned to a sorry situation. He's a deadbeat dad, so his two sons, Brownie and Chumley, were so named after my sister Marcie's two imaginary childhood friends and fairly recently had been left in my care as she had been stationed in Vietnam with the International Red Cross, an assignment she correctly deduced might be harmful to the health, education, and welfare of Brownie and Chumley. The mother of Brownie and Chumley, and the matriarch of the entire Friedman Clan, was Perky. Perky was a small dog who, as so often happens, didn't know she was a small dog. Perky had long ears and a long tail and looked like she'd been put together by a committee. In her eyes, a thousand years of wisdom softly gleamed. Perky had been one of my father's last and closest companions on earth.

If you've been spiritually deprived as a child and are therefore not an animal lover, you may already be in a coma from reading all this. That's good, because I don't care a flea about people who don't love animals. I shall continue my impassioned tale and I shall not stop until the last dog is sleeping.

The last dog was Hank. He looked like one of the flying monkeys in *The Wizard of Oz*, and he didn't understand that the cat could and would hurt him and me and the entire Polish army if we got in her way. Lady was about twenty-two years old and had lived in this house on this ranch almost all of her life, and she didn't need to be growled at by a little dog with a death wish.

So I had the cat hanging down over one side of my face like a purring stalactite, with her whiskers poking into my left nostril, and Hank on the other side, who completely failed to grasp the mortal danger he was placing both of us in by playfully provoking the cat. It was 3:09 in the morning and suddenly a deafening cacophony of barking, hissing, and shrieking erupted, with Lady taking a murderous swat at Hank directly across my fluttering eyelids and Mr. Magoo stepping heavily upon my slumbering scrotum as all of the animals bolted off the bed simultaneously. This invariably signaled the arrival of Dilly, my pet armadillo.

For years Dilly had been showing up in my backyard with the punctuality of a German train. I fed him cat food, dog food, bacon grease—anything. He was a shy, crepuscular, oddly Christlike creature whose arrival brought a measure of comfort to me at the same time that it caused all five dogs to go into attack mode. It's not really necessary to describe what effect this always had on Lady.

After I slipped outside and fed Dilly, I gathered the animals about me like little pieces of my soul. I explained to them once again that Dilly was an old, spiritual friend of mine who was cursed with living in a state full of loud, brash Texans, and we didn't have to make things worse. Somewhere there is a planet, I told them, paraphrasing the great John D. MacDonald, which is inhabited principally by sentient armadillos who occasionally carve up dead human beings and sell them as baskets by the roadside. Perhaps not surprisingly, the animals seemed to relate to this peculiar vision.

Then we all went back to bed and dreamed of fields full of slow-moving rabbits and mice and cowboys and Indians and imaginary childhood friends and tail fins on Cadillacs and girls in the summertime and everything else that time has taken away.

EIGHT

Whenever you leave a given place, even if it's only on a temporary basis, in a great many practical ways you cease to exist in the minds of the people there. This is especially true if the place you leave is called New York City. Some of the people, of course, will stay in touch with you for a while after your departure. The truth is, however, that once you go, you are demoted or upgraded, depending on how you look at it, to the status of an imaginary childhood friend.

Since I firmly believed that e-mail was the work of Satan, I relied heavily upon the telephone to endeavor to maintain what residual threads of relationships remained between myself and my former fellow New Yorkers. None of them, interestingly enough, took the initiative to call me first. This was not terribly surprising. The work that each of them was doing in New York was probably far more important than anything that anyone else in the whole fucking world could possibly be involved with. So I didn't really expect to hear from them. In several cases, I didn't particularly want to hear from them.

So much for the Village Irregulars, I thought. So much for all my loyal Dr. Watsons. I had many friends, or at least some friends, in the beautiful Texas Hill Country, and now, with the cat no longer in charge of the loft, and no longer in the seductive hands of lesbians either, I could very possibly make a new life for myself right back here where I'd started. Ratso and the rest no doubt would not approve. They'd think I'd given up, gone home in defeat, had some kind of metropolis meltdown and returned to the sticks with my tail between my legs. If that's what they wanted to believe, let them, I figured. The opposite was actually true. I'd merely eaten an appropriate amount for my figure. I'd had enough of New York. I didn't expect them to understand this. Some of the most provincial people I'd ever met in my life lived in New York. Some of the most open-minded and progressive people lived in rural, bucolic, out-of-the-way places. How did they survive, I wondered, without art openings? Without Broadway? Without ridiculously overpriced, vertical food restaurants?

Such was my black attitude toward the city that I loved to hate as I walked through the dusty, drafty lodge that chilly Hill Country morning and found that it reminded me very much, and not without a note of fondness, of my loft in little old New York. The fireplace was burning bright as the Friedmans, five dogs and a cat, followed me around from room to room, happy to have me back with them once more. And when I thought about it, I was happy, too.

It was in that mood of happiness and serenity that I wandered into the little private investigator's room with my coffee, cigar, and portable phone and proceeded to blast a large Nixon. All of my adult life I've been consumed with the notion that cigar smoke masks the odor of a dump. That's not the only reason I smoke cigars, of course. It's just a perk. My sister, however, has long maintained that the combined odors of my dumps and my cigars are capable of creating a binary reaction that could blow the toilet lid off the world.

Anyway, it's my first morning back in Texas and I'm blasting a large Nixon and some of the Friedmans have gathered around me in the small, rather dank dumper, sort of like a spectator sport, and there's a huge photo of Amelia Earhart hanging over the dumper and a drawing by the late great cowboy cartoonist Ace Reid of two cowboys in a pickup truck with flood waters coming over the hood and one of them is saying, "I hate to be pessimistic but I've seen some bad droughts start out just like this."

So I'm a Jewish cowboy, you see, and I always carry my large portable phone with me and I only ride two-legged animals. The phone hasn't rung since I've gotten to the ranch, but you never know when you're going to get the call that's going to change your life, or maybe even a call from Cousin Nancy and Tony at the nearby Utopia Rescue Ranch offering to bring breakfast over for the Friedmans and myself. The Friedmans like bacon. They're not really practicing Jews; they're good enough already. At the moment, four of them were watching me take a dump. It was quite a cosmic circumstance in that all four of my current spectators were black. I'm not a racist and I don't care who watches me dump, but it was rather uncanny that Brownie and Hank, the two brown Friedmans, were not in attendance. This phenomenon, the gathering of Gooey, Chumley, Perky, and Fly (our first Rescue Ranch charter member, now adopted by me), was not terribly unusual. My sister Marcie named this intrepid little group the BQS or Black Quadruped Society. Very often you would find all the black Friedmans congregating together, with the brown Friedmans nowhere to be seen. Apparently the Black Quadruped Society had determined at their last meeting that on this particular morning they would gather to watch me have a shit. It was fascinating really, if you thought about it. There are wonderful things to be learned about ourselves from the behavior of animals.

Some people have difficulty shitting if they're being watched, but it's never bothered me. As an entertainer, you get used to having large crowds of people scrutinizing your every move, and pretty soon whatever happens—dumping, fucking, vomiting, attempting suicide—all becomes part of that magical world we call show business. So, having the Friedmans monitor my efforts at stool propulsion was really just another show in my hip pocket. As Willie Nelson once told me, "Just do the best you can and never give 'em everything you've got."

The Black Quadruped Society watched the blue smoke from my cigar drift almost wistfully to the ceiling of the shitter. Their eyes reflected the peace and love of the family primeval, the unconventional, underdog family of my heart. It was a God-made gathering as timeless as the rain; instead of a campfire, there stood a throne. Into this simple, serene, rustic tableau, this little group of solitary spirits sharing the shadows of their souls, came a jangling interruption from the world of modern technology. From its perch high on top of the toilet, the phone was ringing. The Black Quadruped Society looked at the phone and then looked back at me, sitting stolidly on the dumper smoking a cigar. There was nothing wrong with any of this. It was the birth of a nation. It was how the West was won. It was the creation of the heavens and the earth and all the wondrous shit therein.

I reached around to pick up the blower from the back of the dumper, mindful of the recent household accident that had occurred to Dylan Ferrero as he was obliviously wiping his ass. I was able to retrieve the receiver without doing myself physical harm. The Black Quadruped Society was impressed.

"Start talkin'," I said.

"What're you doin'?" said a female voice. I looked at the members of the BQS. The members of the BQS looked solemnly back at me.

"Who wants to know?" I said cautiously.

"How soon we forget," said the voice.

Even individuals who are highly proficient at multitasking can find it fairly dicey sometimes to try to talk to someone on the blower while taking a Nixon. Often evasive procedures are required, at least until the identity of the caller is known, before vouchsafing one's precise locus and the nature of the activity in which one is currently involved.

"Who the fuck is this?" I said, trying for the casually appropriate conversational tone.

"Oh, Jesus. Aren't we the big detective."

Reception on the portable blower was not the best in the dumper, and reception in my gray matter department was not the best in the morning. That having been said, it was a bit unsettling that I still didn't know for sure who the hell it was I was talking to. I have known many women over many years from many aspects of my life, and I have found that their telephone techniques are quite often maddeningly similar. The other problem is if you guess wrong you really look like an idiot. There was also the possibility that, like McGovern, I was going a bit deaf.

"Look, I'm rather busy right now," I said. "I don't really have time to play games."

"What're you doin'?"

"I'm not doing anything," I said. "I'm *trying* to do something."

By this time I was definitely getting a handle on the caller's identity. So many beauties had gone by the boards in my life, hapless victims of time and cocaine and geography. When somebody called me it could be anybody.

"You really *don't* know who I am? That's sad. I'll give you a few hints. I wear the pants in the family. Think Amelia Earhart."

I glanced over my shoulder at the giant framed photo of Amelia standing in front of her plane, dressed in her mannish flight suit. A chill ran up my spine. Was somebody watching me? Was it just a cosmic circumstance or was it merely the routine perversity of life? Had the caller visited my dumper here on the ranch previously? Of course not. That was ridiculous. How could she have known about Amelia? And what did Amelia have to say about all this? That mischievous glint in her eye. That Mona Larry smile. Was she a tomboy? Was she a lesbian? And then, at long last, I had it. It was my upstairs New York neighbor, Winnie Katz.

"Why does your voice sound different?" I said.

"I've just got a cold or something. What *are* you doing? You sound very distracted."

"I'm trying to take a Nixon."

"Thanks for sharing. I had a little different image of you in mind."

"What did you think I was doing? Masturbating like a monkey?"

"No, I just pictured you running around the ranch with your homo helmet on your head playing cowboy or something."

It never failed to set my ears back a bit when I heard a New York lesbian belittling cowboys. It was something that probably shouldn't have bothered me, but it did. Everybody seemed to be picking on cowboys these days. The lesbians. The pointy-headed intellectuals. The goddamn Europeans. It was getting to be a fucking stompede of abuse and it was making me weary in the old spiritual saddle. The cowboy was a dying breed anyway. Why not let us die in peace? The answer is, because they never do. All a cowboy wants is a little bit of elbow room. That's why you don't find many of us in New York. We didn't need to have some lesbo calling cowboy hats "homo helmets." It wasn't even very original. Jimmie Silman, aka Washington Ratso, had been calling cowboy hats homo helmets for at least two decades now. Of course, Ratso had a right to call them anything he wanted, because, like me, he wore one except when he was sleeping or fucking. There's a real cowboy for you, God bless him. But seriously folks, being a cowboy in your mind is as important as babies' heads exiting vaginas or should we say vaginae. The cowboy is one of the last universal shining symbols to the children of the world. Hell, ask Anne Frank. She is believed to have died at Bergen-Belsen at the hands of the people who gave us sauerkraut. Though her body was never found, Anne Frank put a face on the Holocaust by writing her little diary. Sergeant Silverbauer of the SS helped the cause quite obliviously by emptying the contents of the briefcase that contained the diary onto the floor of the secret annex to make room for a set of silver candlestick-holders which this proud SS officer would steal. That was how the diary was found after the war. But something else was found in the secret annex as well. In Anne's little corner of the room there were old photographs of American cowboy stars still fluttering from the walls where she'd left them. God bless the cowboy, I say! And goddamn any New York lesbians or Nazi Europeans who try to belittle him or tarnish his silver lariat of stars.

"What happened, Hopalong? You didn't shit out your brains, did you? I was just calling to tell you in your haste to beat it out of New York you forgot something."

Everything I'd ever loved had already slipped through the slippery fingers of my life, I thought. What could I possibly have forgotten?

"What could I possibly have forgotten?"

"Your wallet," she said. "I found it on the floor of your loft."

NINE

As I coaxed Winnie into remaining on the line, I vowed never again to bring the blower into the dumper. It was only asking for trouble. My attempts at laying some decent cable had been totally thwarted by the call, and now, with the phone to my ear and with my jeans still around my ankles, I hopped like Hopalong Cassidy into the nearby Indian Ghost Room to determine if my wallet happened to be residing in a previously worn pant. Once I had the answer, I planned to hop right back to the dumper and resume the congressional hearing. What complicated this plan a bit was that the Black Quadruped Society, now joined by Brownie, Hank, and Lady, were all following my white luminous buttocks in single file into the Indian Ghost Room.

"What the hell do you think this is?" I shouted. "The Macy's Thanksgiving Day Parade?"

"What're you doin'?" asked Winnie.

"You wouldn't believe me if I told you."

"Try me."

"No!"

I couldn't really blame the Friedmans. They hadn't seen me in a long time and they wanted to be with me. For that matter, I wanted to be with them. I just didn't want to be hopping around with my pants down, talking to a lesbian in New York, with all of them following me like the Pied Piper of Medina. That's Texas, not Saudi Arabia.

"Where are you now?"

"I'm in the Ghost Room—"

"The what?"

"Indian Ghost Room. It's a long stultifyingly dull story. I'm searching for my previously worn pant. Ah-ha! There it is. Give me some room, will you?"

"Who are you talking to?"

"Never end a sentence in a preposition. The grammatically correct way to say that is, 'Who are you talking to, asshole?'"

"You took the words right out of my mouth. Who *are* you talking to, asshole?"

"I'm talking to a Russian peasant with a withered arm."

"You sure you're not masturbating?"

"I'm looking for my goddamn wallet."

"I already told you. I found it on the floor of your loft when I was bringing in your mail. I put it on your desk. You want me to FedEx it to you?"

"It's not my wallet."

"Whose wallet do you think it is?"

"I'm holding my wallet in my hand! You see? It's right here. Right, everybody?"

"Who are you talking to?"

"I'm talking to a large, extended Pakistani family that came over to borrow some nuclear weapons. You see, everybody? There's my driver's license. No, that's not Sirhan Sirhan. That's me. That's my name. I did *not* forget my wallet!"

"So what's a strange wallet doing in your loft? Hey! This could be a big case for a private dick like you. 'The Mystery of the Missing Wallet.' Your fans will stay away in droves."

By this time I was hopping back into the dumper with many of the Friedmans mistakenly thinking it was some new kind of game, leaping up into the air, blocking my path, and pawing playfully at my scrotum. Finally, I sat back down on the throne and politely asked Winnie if she'd go back down to my loft and get the mystery wallet and call me back. She agreed, I thought, rather grudgingly, hanging up as I was still speaking to her. Moments later, I had completed my morning ablutions. Amelia Earhart appeared to be leering malevolently at me as I goose-stepped out of the dumper.

Winnie took her sweet Sapphic time to call me back. This gave me the opportunity to do a little quick deductive reasoning regarding this curious situation. There had been several rather rowdy farewell parties at the loft in the days preceding my departure. McGovern had brought what had looked like a Gray Line Tour of individuals into my place, none of whom I had ever seen before in my life. Could McGovern or one of his drunken acquaintances have dropped his wallet? Of course. That had to be the answer.

I put the matter out of my mind, made a pot of Kona coffee, and fired up my second cigar of the morning, an Epicure Number 2. What would I do without the Hawaiians and the Cubans? I thought. Probably miss out on a lot of the flavor and the smoke of life, I figured. I took the cup of steaming coffee and the cigar and walked outside the lodge with the Friedmans into the bright, frosty Hill Country morning. Now that I wasn't in New York, I reflected, having nothing to do wasn't so bad.

Yet, almost like a locked-room puzzle, the affair of the strange, intrusive wallet kept niggling at the corner of my consciousness. Was I so scattered when I left the city that I hadn't noticed it? Very possibly. Well, we'd know the answer soon. Hell, I thought, it probably belonged to McGovern. He could lose his wallet for several years and never be aware of it. That was one of the beautiful things about McGovern.

I was sitting on the old round picnic table with the Friedmans, just looking at the hills surrounding me, when the blower made its presence known again. Why did I even have a blower anymore? As Groucho Marx told me once by way of introduction, "I've already met everybody I want to meet." He also gave me this sage advice when I met him, grudgingly as it was, in New York: "Go back to Texas." It had taken me a while, but I now agreed with Groucho on both counts.

"Start talkin'," I said.

"Okay, I'm in your loft. It smells like a cigar died in here. But you're right. It's not your wallet."

"Good. For a moment I was afraid I was living in a parallel universe."

"It belongs to a guy named Robert Scalopini. Know him?"

"I think I met him once on a chafing dish. Of course I don't know him. I don't even want to know him. He's probably one of those guys McGovern dragged in before I left town. Things got a little crazy."

"So what do you want me to do with the wallet?"

"Look, Winnie, I know you're busy, but I'm in Texas right now. Just handle it, will you? Call the guy. Call the cops. Call the Missing Wallet Bureau."

"Sure, Sherlock," she said scornfully. "What are neighbors for?"

TEN

That afternoon I took the six Friedmans for a long walk around the ranch, leaving Lady by herself at the lodge to enjoy a little peace and quiet. I don't know whether or not you've noticed this interesting phenomenon, but it's been my observation that cats always seem to be outnumbered in this world. Cats are Indians. Cats are Jews. Cats are Negroes with the blues. Cats are poets when they choose. Of course, sometimes cats just like to snooze. We left Lady lying on a warm chair by the fire, looking like a lovely piece of living architecture.

I took the Friedmans out on the South Flat and over to Big Foot Falls, so named after Big Foot Wallace, a frontier scout who lived with the Indians. I took the Friedmans down Armadillo Canyon, so named because God saw his first armadillos there. He e-mailed Noah just in time to get the little boogers aboard the ark. Then God took a power nap for about five thousand years and woke up just in time to speak to Pat Robertson.

The Friedmans loved to go on walks. They even loved the word "walk." I liked to go on walks, too. Sometimes they almost gave you a chance to think. After all these years, I didn't have my name on peb-

51

bled glass. I didn't have a beautiful, leggy secretary. Ratso was right. There was good reason to be depressed. Without a case to work on, I had very little to justify my existence on this planet. Ratso, to be fair, had tried his best to bolster my self-confidence by extolling the glories of the past. But I didn't really believe in yesterday. It was just another small town too far off the superhighway to bother with.

The only wisp of a mystery in the air, I reflected as we hiked up the back side of Echo Hill toward the crystal beds, was how that wallet had gotten into my loft. Was I slipping? In my haste to bugout for the dugout could I have missed something like that? It had to have been accidentally dropped by one of McGovern's buddies from the Corner Bistro. They had been fairly heavily monstered that night. For that matter, so had I. What the hell, I thought. Let Winnie handle it. Now that she was taking a sabbatical from her dance classes, she had plenty of time on her hands. She wasn't busy like me, watching the Friedmans pore over the site of the old dump. More than fifty years, shit had been crammed into that hole in the ground and burned repeatedly. The Friedmans ran back and forth over the dump excitedly like they knew something they weren't telling me, which was very possible. Mr. Magoo hiked his leg and whizzed on an old archery target. Perky was sniffing curiously at the remains of an ancient tennis shoe. Somewhere down there were half-burned relics of a bygone age, camp newspapers, menus, letters from home, written by those whose names were now written in the stars. This is how all of civilization was built, I thought. The shining city rises from the old Echo Hill dump.

"Gentlemen," I said to the Friedmans. "And ladies, of course. Behold the future of man!"

The Friedmans looked at me rather quizzically. Then Mr. Magoo hiked his leg and whizzed on what was left of a bright-red plastic kayak.

By the time we got back to the lodge, all of us were exhausted. I made the Friedmans some bones and I made myself some coffee and, so she wouldn't feel left out, I opened a can of tuna for Lady, which she stared at briefly with a slightly bemused expression on her face before following something near the ceiling with her eyes that neither the dogs nor I could see. This was a recent and fairly unnerving habit of Lady's and, to my mind, it invariably brought on the notion of impending doom. How accurate an assessment this was I will leave to you, gentile reader, to decide. I'm a fatalist. I'm ready for anything. That's probably why it never happens.

I put a few more logs on the fire, then walked a cup of coffee and a freshly stoked cigar into the Ghost Room, where I stared down the answering machine. It blinked first. There were three messages. The first was Cousin Nancy wanting to know if I'd like to have dinner with them at the Rescue Ranch. The second was from my beautiful and brilliant friend Dr. Noreena Hertz in London. Unfortunately, her British accent was so thick I could never understand more than half of what she had to say. Maybe that was why we got along. The third was from McGovern. He sounded highly agitato so I called him back first.

"MIT! MIT! MIT!" he said. That was our international man-in-trouble secret code. McGovern, of course, began most of his calls to me that way.

"MIT!" I said, somewhat peevishly. Now that I was in the real world of Texas, I didn't feel I had a lot of time for this nonsense. Not that I was doing much of anything else.

"Twenty-four Hours to Die."

"Say what?"

"That's the headline," said McGovern ebulliently. "Twenty-four Hours to Die."

"What headline?"

"The headline of the story I'm writing for the *Daily News.*"

"What's it about? The life span of the fruit fly? Hollywood love affairs?"

"No, it's about the fourth guy getting murdered here in New York. Remember I told you about those three murder victims in the Village? Well, a fourth guy got croaked yesterday."

"So what? There's plenty more where they came from."

"What's the matter with you, Kink? Don't you care anymore?"

"Give me a break, McGovern. I'm down here on vacation. This isn't exactly man bites dog, you know. Millions of people live in the city. Some of them are bound to get taken off the board."

"Are you kidding? There's never been a murder spree like this in the Village. The cops are playing it very close to the vest to avoid setting off a panic. But four victims inside a week and a half? That's big news. Four victims! It's almost like the killer knew you were leaving town, Sherlock."

"Don't try to put me up on a pedestal, Watson."

"I'm kidding, Kink. But you've got to admit it is a big story."

"The big story is your department, Watson. The mind of the killer is my department. Did all the murders take place in the West Village?"

"I thought you'd never ask. No. Two of them took place in the East Village and two of them happened in the West Village."

"Symmetry, Watson, symmetry. This appeals to me. This sense of balance in an unbalanced mind."

"Glad to hear it. Well, I've got to get started on 'Twenty-four Hours to Die.' I'm planning to chronicle the last twenty-four hours in the life of the most recent victim."

"Wonderful, Watson, wonderful! Your industrious nature is a credit to the information age! Pray what is the name of this fourth victim, this unfortunate fellow you are soon to immortalize?"

"Let's see. I had it here somewhere. Here it is. His name is Robert Scalopini."

ELEVEN

One of the hazards to smoking that is seldom talked about is the danger—which fortunately happens only very rarely—of swallowing your cigar. In my whole life it's manifested itself on only one or two occasions, until now, of course. Still holding the portable blower and listening to McGovern yammering on, I walked rather briskly into the kitchen and poured a Texas-sized shot of Jameson's into a glass that was bigger than Dallas. I could still hear McGovern's distant voice buzzing like a malarial mosquito in the background as I threw the contents of the glass in the general direction of my uvula. It went down like a male prostitute at the corner of Truth and Vermouth.

"Did you say Robert Scalopini?" I said at last.

"That's right. Robert Scalopini. Know him?"

"I've seen him on a chafing dish," I said, my mind whirring like a wood-chipper.

"Sounded like you knew him."

"No, McGovern. I didn't know him."

"You don't have to bite my head off. You don't have to sound so peevish. It merely seemed as if you were unsure as to whether or not you knew him."

"Let's just put it this way, McGovern," I said, doing everything in my power to conceal my irritation. "A large, loud, rather inebriated Irishman named Mike McGovern brought a group of his new best friends whom he'd just met, apparently, at the Corner Bistro I believe, to my loft to tell me goodbye at the precise moment I was contemplating committing suicide by jumping through a ceiling fan."

"Go on," said McGovern, somewhat belligerently.

"Someone in your intrepid little group of comrades evidently dropped his wallet in my loft. I have this information on good authority from Winnie Katz, who found said wallet when she was bringing in some mail for me earlier today."

"Go on," said McGovern truculently.

"The wallet, according to Winnie, appears to belong to someone you know. Or should I say *knew*."

"Let's see. Is it Judge Crater's wallet? Is it Frederick Exley's wallet? Is it Jesus Christ's wallet? Uh, Richard Milhous Nixon's wallet?"

"Oh, no, no, my dear Watson! How very witty of you! They've all no doubt been in my loft at one time or another, I feel certain. But none of them, my dear friend, happens to be the party that left his wallet at the—uh—party. That would be someone who, I'm given to believe, had twenty-four hours to live. Or rather, as some might sensationalize the matter, to die."

"What?" said McGovern sharply.

"That's right, Watson. The wallet in my loft belonged to good ol' Bob Scalopini. The late Bob Scalopini, if I'm not mistaken."

Now, of course, it was McGovern's turn to swallow his cigar, except for the fact he didn't smoke cigars. Maybe he would inhale a large, well-twisted joint or an entire Vodka McGovern or those fucking cookies he was incessantly baking. At any rate he must have inhaled something because he didn't speak for a very long while. When I at last heard his voice again, it had an entirely different-sounding resonance. McGovern, a journalist to the core, apparently felt he had a scoop.

"This is unbelievable!" he shouted. "It's a goddamn bird's nest on the ground! And you don't remember which one was Scalopini?"

"Of course not, McGovern. I wasn't the one who brought them over to my loft."

"That's right. But he was definitely there?"

"After applying my methods of deductive reasoning to the known facts in this matter, I must concur, Watson, with your invariably brilliant conclusion."

"Okay, this is great! This is a gift! I've got to get started."

"Watson, life is a gift. Death is a gift. Friendship can even be a gift—"

By this time, however, in his journalistic zeal to follow a hot story, McGovern had already cradled the blower. I could imagine him with his trusty little newspaper reporter's notebook in his hand, burning up the wires, legging it out the door, and always, always, asking an infinite stream of questions, which, of course, led inexorably to further questions and sometimes, possibly, some answers. That's what we all were looking for, of course. Answers. In puzzles. In people. In life. That's why we buy newspapers, why we play the jukebox, why we climb tall mountains, why we squint at a bleb of walrus semen through a microscope, why we go to New York, why we come back to Texas.

Twenty-four hours to die, I thought. That might be more than most of us needed.

TWELVE

The next few days on the ranch were filled with activity. The boys and girls who thronged the little green valley of summertime were gone, of course. So were the hummingbirds. But the three donkeys, Roy, Gabby, and Little Jewford, came by the lodge to visit rather often, always provoking an explosion of barking and excitement on the part of the Friedmans. I kept the fire in the old fireplace burning twenty-four hours a day. To paraphrase Earl Buckelew, I burned wood like a widow woman. I had a good reason for doing so. In my soul I could feel the warmth of the world slipping away.

How could people live, I wondered, without a fire burning brightly in the fireplace? How could they live in an empty loft without a cat dumping vindictively about the floor, or a lesbian dance class pounding relentlessly on the ceiling? How could people live anywhere in this world without Cuban cigars or Kona coffee? How, indeed, could they live at all? I didn't have any answers, but then I didn't have all that many questions either. Most of the time I seemed to just watch the fire, as men had done for thousands of years, all in the twinkle of an eye.

The days passed. Two of them to be exact. I was sitting in the comfortable chair by the fire that Perky and I fought over constantly, half-dreaming of climbing Ayers Rock in Australia with Miss Texas. It doesn't matter. Very little does, actually, once it starts to get smaller and smaller in the rearview mirror of your late-model, four-wheeled penis. It's only later, in your dreams, when it starts to get bigger and bigger and the wheels fall off of your four-wheeled penis, and then your penis gets bigger and bigger, and soon you need a big chair by the fire just for your penis, and you and your penis and Perky are all constantly fighting over that chair. At any rate, it was into this bucolic idyll that a note of modern-day reality intruded by way of the blower.

"Rear Admiral Rumphumper," I said. "How can I hump you? I mean, how can I *help* you?"

"You can help me by never answering the phone that way for the rest of your life."

It was a familiar-sounding male voice with a New York accent. The voice carried with it a strong sense of authority. In fact, if I wasn't mistaken, it was the voice of authority itself. It was my old sometimes friend, sometimes nemesis, Detective Sergeant Mort Cooperman of the NYPD. Now why in the hell would he be calling me in Texas? I wondered.

"Have you seen the papers, Tex?"

"I've seen the *Times*. The *Kerrville Times*, that is. I've seen the *Mountain Sun*. I've seen the *Bandera Bulletin*. I've seen the papers Willie Nelson uses to roll his dope with. They're bigger than the menu at the Carnegie Deli. Of course everything's bigger in Texas."

I don't know why I always derived such unbridled joy out of irritating Cooperman. He was, after all, just a public servant doing his job. A trifle overzealously sometimes, but what the hell. Anyway, my remarks appeared to have hit home. There was a longer than usual silence on the line. Then Cooperman's growl started once again to chew on my ear.

"Tex, I don't have a lot of time for this horseshit, so pull your lips together a minute, will you? Don't start with me, Tex, or I may have to finish with you and you ain't gonna like it. The paper I'm talkin' about is the *Daily News,* which I realize you don't get down there in Texas but I thought maybe your pal McGovern would've told you."

"Told me what?" I said, playing dumb. It achieved no good purpose to get Cooperman really agitated. I just liked to tweak him a little like Tweety Bird used to do to Puddy Tat in those cartoons that kids used to watch before video games came along to suck, fuck, and cajole the innocence out of everybody's childhood. More than anything else, Cooperman, I suppose, reminded me of Yosemite Sam.

"Quite a party you guys had, according to McGovern's story. Guy comes to your place, twenty-four hours later he's dead and you've bolted town for Texas."

"Is that how you found me? McGovern gave you the number?"

"I've always had your number, Tex. But, now that you asked, no, we didn't get your number from McGovern. We went to your loft, just like this murder victim number four did. We thought about getting a search warrant, but then we thought maybe we'd try to talk to you first. We were just getting tired of waiting when we ran into a friendly neighbor who lives upstairs and said she was looking after things for you. She gave us your phone number down there in Texas."

"All my little helpers."

"That's right. Now we need you to help us, Tex. She told us how she found the dead guy's wallet in your loft. What gives?"

"Look, Sergeant. I wouldn't know a Robert Scalopini if I stepped on one."

"You seem to know his name pretty well. I never mentioned the victim's name to you."

"Of course I know his name," I said, taking my turn at becoming irritable. "McGovern told me his name and so did Winnie."

"Winnie Katz, isn't it? That your girlfriend?"

Sometimes in life you just had to take a few deep breaths and pretend you were a Buddhist or a dead teenager or something. When you banter with a cop you've got to be very careful you don't cross that police line.

"She's one of New York's finest lesbians," I said at last.

"Yeah, I thought I picked up something about her. So she finds the stiff's wallet on the floor of your loft. That doesn't look good. So I feel compelled to ask you again, Tex. How'd it get there?"

"How the hell do I know? Look, Sergeant, I didn't kill the guy. I didn't know the guy. As near as I can recall, I never met the guy. Maybe McGovern remembers more than he told me."

"That's the problem I have, Tex. Your pal McGovern doesn't remember meeting the guy either. He says he thinks he brought a few people over to your place, but he doesn't know if this bird was one of them."

"If McGovern's the one who in all likelihood brought this guy over to my loft, why don't you try to refresh *his* memory? Why don't you ask *him* these questions?"

"Because the stiff's wallet didn't turn up on the floor of *his* apartment. It turned up on the floor of *your* apartment. Capisce?"

There exists a certain thing called "cop logic" that never fails to boggle the rational mind. Sure, there were cases that had boggled Cooperman's mind, that were eventually, sometimes with great media fanfare, resolved by the Kinkster. Yet there were also times when Cooperman and I had worked together with good results. Why then would he waste both of our time grilling me as if I were his main suspect, making me not eager to want to help him, making me crazy? So they found a dead guy's wallet in my loft. Big fucking deal.

"Look, Sergeant," I said, "I've already told you I never met this guy. I never met his wallet—"

"Understand me, Tex. If you don't refresh your memory about this guy being in your loft, as McGovern's story claims he was, things could get even worse for you. Tex, I want you up here tomorrow at the precinct."

"Sergeant, be reasonable. I'm down here in Texas and Texas is a very big state. If I left for the airport now I couldn't be sure I'd get there tomorrow."

"Okay, pal. You have forty-eight hours. If you're not here by then—"

"You don't really believe I croaked this guy?"

"If you're not here by then, I'll issue a material witness warrant to your local sheriff. He's probably the guy from *Gunsmoke,* but you can bet your ass, Tex, he'll bring you in."

"Jesus Christ."

"If he had a wallet, I'd bring him in, too."

THIRTEEN

I was mad at McGovern, mad at Winnie, mad at the whole damn world. I was just starting to relax and unwind my catfish here in Texas and now the horse manure had really hit the fan. I didn't know for sure how the wallet had gotten into the loft, but, if I were a betting man, I'd put my money on McGovern bringing over the flotsam and jetsam of the Corner Bistro without even knowing the identities of the individuals. McGovern, who'd once combed his hair before meeting a racehorse, was a trusting soul. This time, he'd gone too far. Compounding his error in judgment, he'd then seen fit to write up the whole *megilla* in the *Daily News*. Why couldn't he just have left it alone? I didn't know the stiff. I couldn't have picked him out of a lineup. What could I possibly bring to Cooperman's table by hustling my buttocks back to New York? I hadn't, of course, read McGovern's article, but I could just imagine how much he must have embellished the situation to have Cooperman so hot on my trail. And Winnie'd been some help, as well. Making it possible for her local law enforcement officer to easily get in touch with me. Telling him she'd found the stiff's wallet in my loft. Hell yes, it sounded bad. And here I was, not knowing the victim, not knowing how his fucking wallet had gotten into my loft, innocent as the Baby Jesus, just trying to sit by the fire and watch the Fox News Network twenty-four hours a day. That's what happens when you mind your own business. In a growing rage, I called McGovern's number.

"MIT! MIT! MIT! You fuckhead!" I shouted.

"Who's calling, please?"

"McGovern, what the hell did you *say* in that story you wrote?"

"You mean 'Twenty-four Hours to Die'?"

"In twenty-four hours I'm going to kill *your* ass."

"What are you so upset about? I just told the truth. The piece has gotten great response."

"I'm aware of that. Sergeant Cooperman just called me."

"Cooperman called you? At the ranch?"

"That's right. And he wasn't looking for Gabby Hayes. I think my good friend Winnie Katz aided and abetted him in locating me. And, of course, the catalyst for the whole thing was your ridiculous story."

"I just wrote the truth!"

"You know what the Turks say? They say, 'When you tell the truth, have one foot in the stirrup.'"

"You *had* one foot in the stirrup, Kink. You just didn't ride far enough. Cooperman just probably wants to ask you a few questions. That's all. There's no reason to get so excited."

"Look, Cooperman doesn't just want to ask questions. Cooperman wants answers. Answers I ain't got. If you listen to Cooperman, it sounds like he thinks I croaked the guy. Now where would he get an idea like that?"

There was a long silence on the line. I knew McGovern wouldn't deliberately put me in a bad situation. But that appeared to be exactly what he'd done and we both knew it. The truth was the truth, of course. But what the hell was the truth? I wanted the answer to that one as much as McGovern.

"Let's look at this rationally," said McGovern. "Let's apply a little deductive reasoning, like your imaginary childhood friend Sherlock would do if he were here."

"He is here."

"Okay. Neither of us put the wallet of a murder victim in your loft, so the guy himself must've dropped it there just before he got himself croaked."

"Considerate of him."

"The point is, I think I know which one he was. There were only three guys that followed me to your place, and I think the tall, skinny one was Scalopini. It had to be him or else how'd the wallet get dropped there? So it was accurate to say that the victim, not realizing he had twenty-four hours to die, attended a party at Kinky Friedman's loft."

I didn't know whether to kill myself or get a haircut. It was like somebody had hit me on the head with a hammer. I could've shit standing. My thoughts were swirling around like a Texas blue norther. For one of the few times in my life, I was totally at a loss for words.

"Kink. Kink? Are you there?"

I was there, all right. I was here and I was there and I was everywhere I didn't want to be. The whole scenario, I reflected, was positively Kafkaesque. By leaving New York when I did, I'd given the appearance of being more involved than if I'd stayed. Guilt was a funny thing. It had a peculiar nasty little habit of attaching itself to you, of washing all over you, even when you knew in your heart you were blameless as you were the day you were born.

Being Jewish, of course, never cuts you much slack in the guilt department. It didn't help that half the city of New York was reading with interest and raising a collective eyebrow at the news that its latest murder victim had been hanging out socially at the Kinkster's loft just hours before his unfortunate demise. Certainly, Cooperman was curious. As for myself? The great detective didn't have a clue. I was, however, rapidly running out of charm. So I hustled the still-protesting McGovern off the blower and rounded up Rambam.

"Secret bat phone."

"Yeah. I think I've got a problem."

"Problems R Us. What happened? You get stuck fucking a cow?"

"Rambam, this is serious. Did you see McGovern's piece in the *Daily News?*"

"Who hasn't? Remind me never to go to a party at your loft."

"It *wasn't* a party. I was the host, supposedly, and I hardly remember being there myself."

"Those are the best kind. When people say you had a good time."

"Well, I'm not having a good time now. Cooperman just called me."

"He called you at the ranch?"

"No, Rambam. He called me at my chalet in Gstaad and the call was then beamed by satellite over to me here at the ranch."

"Cooperman actually called you at the ranch. How'd he get the number?"

"He came prowling around Vandam Street, apparently, after he'd read McGovern's wonderful story. He ran into Winnie Katz, apparently, grilled her, and she, like any good citizen, gave him the wallet and, apparently, my number."

"Lot of apparentlys. Bottom line is, never trust a lesbian."

"Now you tell me."

"Never trust anybody else either. Okay, Cooperman's already got the wallet. What else does he want?"

"That's what's worrying me a bit. He wants my ass back in New York yesterday. To be more precise, he gave me forty-eight hours."

"Wow. Twenty-four hours to die. Forty-eight hours to get back to New York. Working with a lot of time lines here. What did Cooperman say would happen if you decide not to come back?"

"He'll call the local sheriff, he says. Have me brought back."

"A material witness warrant probably. Well, don't ever say you're not wanted. Reading between the lines, I'd say somebody's just cut in on your little Texas two-step."

"Meaning?"

"Meaning your vacation's over before it started. You've heard about the long arm of the law? This one is reaching out to grab you by the balls, brother. You don't mess around with a material witness warrant. They'll find you and bring you back, believe me. And don't forget, right now you're just a material witness. Cooperman could easily upgrade you at any time."

"Meaning?"

"Meaning you could go from a material witness to a target of the investigation at any time. You could, depending on circumstances, even be upgraded to a suspect. The nomenclature's fairly meaningless to the world in general, of course, but in the eyes of a cop, it can be very finely nuanced. This probably won't happen, but the other thing you could be is 'a person of interest.' That's the one you *really* don't want any part of. Cooperman didn't mention a search warrant, did he?"

"Not that I remember."

"Then you can assume he got one and they've already been through the place. There's nothing terribly incriminating there probably. They could've found some long-forgotten stashes of dope left behind by one of your halfwit friends like Chinga or McGovern. Maybe there's an overdue library book from 1957."

"In 1957 I was attending Edgar Allan Poe Elementary School in Houston, Texas."

"Okay. So it was planted."

Still talking to Rambam, I got up from the cozy chair by the fire and walked into the kitchen and poured myself another cup of Kona coffee. I opened the cabinet and looked at a bottle of Jameson's for a moment, then closed the cabinet door. Funny how I didn't seem to be drinking as much these days. Dealing with the NYPD, of course, could drive you to drink.

"Look," I said finally to Rambam, "I didn't kill anybody. I didn't conceal any evidence of a crime. So why do I feel just a weensy bit guilty?"

"Two reasons," said Rambam. "One is all the pressure you're feeling from Cooperman, and two is because you're a fucking Jew. Quite normal, under the circumstances."

"So I guess I just come back and face the music."

"There's no other option. And believe me, the music you'll probably face is going to sound like it's coming from a jukebox in hell. It'll make you wish you were listening to Barry Manilow."

I hung up with Rambam and went back into the living room and looked at the fire. For some reason the words of an old cowboy song came into my head. "I'm Going to Leave Ol' Texas Now / They've got no use for the longhorned cow / They've plowed and fenced my cattle range / And the people there are all so strange."

I walked closer to the fire and thought I might just relax a moment before I began the tedium of making last-minute plane reservations. I started to sit down, but then I realized that would not be possible. Perky was already curled up comfortably in my chair.

FOURTEEN

Just like a hospital, a bus station, or a whorehouse has its own institutionalized ambience, so, indubitably, does a cop shop. I waited in the hallway, seated in one of those ubiquitous plastic chairs in which so many troubled souls had waited before me. The real bad guys get to go right in, no doubt. It's just the guys like me, the ones who might be on their way to becoming persons of interest, in whom the cops seem to have almost no interest at all. I thought about all of this and wished that I could still be fighting Perky for the chair by the fire.

By this time, I'd gotten over my anger at McGovern and Winnie. To paraphrase my father, they were just people doing the best they could. Given the same set of circumstances, if I'd been in their places, I might have done the same. And besides, this was America and I had nothing to worry about because I was innocent of any crime related to murder or stolen wallets. I wasn't totally innocent, of course. I'd let some good people down in my time. I broke some beautiful hearts that it was too late to mend. I almost ritually bought bad aloha shirts in Hawaii. (Somebody had to buy them.) I wasn't perfect. But I wasn't as guilty as Cooperman seemed to be making me out to be. In fact, I wasn't guilty at all. Unless being human is being guilty. You could argue that one, of course. If you wanted to.

While I sat there cops came and went, all on their busy little errands. Some of them glanced at me. Some of them didn't bother. None of them said, "Good morning." Of course it wasn't really morning anymore. It had been when I'd gotten there. It was now a few hairs and a freckle past Gary Cooper time and I was still waiting in this fucking plastic chair. Ah well, I thought, like the Guinness slogan says: "Good things happen to those who wait." Bad things happen, too, of course.

At least the time I sat there gave me a chance to get my story down. My story was that Scalopini, or whatever the hell his name was, had come over with McGovern and a few other guys I didn't know on the night before I'd left town. They were all fairly heavily monstered when they got there, and by the end of the evening I was pretty well walking on my knuckles as well. The soon-to-be-dead guy must've dropped his wallet on the floor at some time during the visit and was too fucked up to notice its absence. Of course, the rest of us had also been too fucked up to notice its presence. Maybe it had fallen against the counter or underneath the desk. Maybe we'd kicked it around like a soccer ball for a few hours. How the hell did I know? Anyway, I never saw it there. Then I left for Texas. That was my story and I was sticking to it.

"Hey, Tex," said a familiar voice. "Come on in. Didn't realize you'd been waiting in the green room so long. Sorry 'bout that. Been a ball-dragger of a day and it hasn't even started yet."

The voice and, of course, the vessel that housed it belonged to none other than Detective Sergeant Buddy Fox, a man not often known for being this positively chatty. His tone and demeanor were friendly, conversational, almost breezy, a far cry from Cooperman's blunt, bullying, doom-and-gloom telephone technique. Was an incipient case of good cop–bad cop already taking form? Why bother with such a charade for a guy like me? I wondered. Hell, I wasn't even a person of interest yet. Or was I?

"Thanks for coming back so fast, Tex," said Fox, as he led me down a long, cramped corridor and ushered me into a small, drab room, the only other occupants of which appeared to be filing cabinets. "Myself, I've wanted to go on a vacation ever since the day I first put on a badge. I try like hell, but I can't get away. Know why, Tex?"

"Why?"

"Because the poor miserable bastards that make up the human race keep on killing each other. They're probably doing it just to keep me from taking the family to Sea World. I haven't had a vacation in thirty years. Kids are all grown up. Don't even want to go to Sea World. I'm the only one who wants to go to Sea World. But the bastards keep killing each other."

"That's tough."

"Go ahead and smoke, Tex, if you like. I'm going to. If we can't kill somebody else we might as well kill ourselves. Right?"

"Right," I said. I pulled out a cigar and lopped the butt off. Before I could light it, Fox, like some thoughtful waiter, fired up his Zippo and did the honors for me. Then he lit his cigarette. Fox inhaled, then exhaled extravagantly—and rather sadly, I thought, as if he were losing the smoke of life.

"Mort'll be here in a minute," said Fox lightly. "Go easy on him, Tex. He's pretty grumpy today."

"Maybe he needs a trip to Sea World."

"Maybe," said Fox. He didn't say anything else for a while. He just looked straight ahead, as if attempting to establish eye contact with a nearby filing cabinet.

The little room seemed to noticeably darken when Cooperman finally made his entrance. He carried with him the now-several-days-old *Daily News* opened to McGovern's story with the bold headline "Twenty-four Hours to Die." He tossed the paper to me and hoisted his large body onto a desk.

"Read it," was all he said.

I pored over the piece dutifully. There was a photo of Scalopini that seemed to vaguely resemble one of the three wise men McGovern had dragged to my loft, but I really couldn't be sure. He'd apparently not been a model citizen. He'd done some time more than twenty years ago on sexual assault charges involving a young girl. Since getting out of prison eight years ago, he'd worked on and off as a bouncer, a shoe salesman, and a limo driver. He'd been married and divorced twice. And, of course, on the last night of his life, he'd stopped by to pay a social visit to Kinky Friedman's loft. There wasn't much else to it. There didn't have to be.

"Is that the guy?" growled Cooperman. "Guy who came to your party?"

"It wasn't a party. I didn't—"

"Is that the guy?"

"I think it's him. I can't really be sure."

"You *think* it's him. What else do you *think*?"

"Not too much," I said, looking doubtfully down at the guy's picture in the paper.

Suddenly, something struck me in the chest, startling me out of whatever protective stupor you habitually fall into whenever you're being grilled by cops. It didn't really hurt. It just surprised me a little. I saw what it was quickly enough and caught it in my hands. It was the guy's wallet.

"Now I know what it's like," I said, "to be struck by a speeding wallet."

"You seen it before?" asked Cooperman sharply, all no-nonsense now.

"Never," I said. "The guy must've dropped it—"

"At the party you didn't have?"

"Look, Sergeant, I didn't invite these guys over. I didn't want to see them. I didn't even want to see McGovern."

"Take a good look at that wallet. Look at his driver's license. Is-that-the-guy?"

"I guess it must've been him."

"You guess it must've been him? You *guess* it must've been him? Never seen the wallet?"

"No."

"Want to know how he died?"

"Sure. Tell me."

"Tell him, Fox."

"Bound and gagged with his dick cut off. Bled to death. Slowly."

The room grew quiet. I looked at the guy's driver's license photo again. It wasn't a bad shot, as they go. Didn't look much like the picture in the *Daily News,* but then you never should believe everything you see in the papers. What the hell was I doing here anyway? I wondered.

"Think carefully, Tex," snarled Cooperman. "You've never laid eyes on that wallet before?"

"Never," I repeated truthfully, wondering why Cooperman was being so persistent. Where the hell was he going with this?

I didn't get to find out right away because Cooperman's wallet fetish was interrupted by a sharp knock on the door. A uniform came in and handed Cooperman some papers. He perused them with a grave expression, then abruptly removed his large buttocks from the desk.

"Looks like a fifth victim, Tex. Went down in Chelsea very late last night. This one was found with a knitting needle jammed up his nose right into his brain."

"What'll they think of next?" said Fox.

"You got in this morning, right, Tex?" said Cooperman.

"That's right. I took a cab from the airport to here, just stopping long enough at my place to drop off my busted valise."

"We've got to get over to Chelsea now, but I want you to understand something, Tex. Under no circumstances are you to leave the city. You got that?"

"What am I?" I said. "A witness? A suspect?"

Cooperman looked at me coldly with obsidian eyes that had seen a lot of shit go down in this city and were sure that they were going to see a lot more. He smiled a smile that wasn't really a smile; it was a stubborn, bitter rictus of malice.

"What are you?" he asked mockingly. "You are whatever we want you to be. 'Cause I'll let you in on a little secret, Tex. Your friend McGovern got it wrong. This dead guy? Scalopini?"

"Dickless wonder," said Fox. Cooperman paid him no attention.

"This dead guy? Scalopini?" he repeated. "He was never at your loft. He wasn't even in the city that night. He was on a skiing trip in Vermont. When he came back the next day, the killer surprised him when he entered his own apartment. I'll take that wallet now."

I looked down at the wallet in my hand. Then I gave it to Cooperman.

"Then how—?" I started to ask.

"That's what we want to know," said Cooperman.

FIFTEEN

Much later that afternoon, at the Second Avenue Deli, Ratso's large, slightly pear-shaped, Jewish buttocks were literally on the edge of his seat as I regaled him with the morning's adventures at the cop shop. Cop-talk about "vics" and "perps" always seemed to titillate Ratso's proclivities to delve deeply into the psychological nature of the criminal mind. But unfortunately, or perhaps fortunately, depending upon the way you looked at it, Ratso was quintessentially a good guy. And good guys rarely if ever are capable of gleaning significant insights into the criminal mind. Nevertheless, Ratso's enthusiasm often compensated for his spiritual disability.

"This is it, baby!" he shouted, as the waiter brought the matzo ball soup. "This is the big case we've been waiting for, Sherlock!"

"It also has the advantage," I said, "of my being involved in it whether I like it or not."

Ratso, never one to pick up on ironical nuances, or nuances of any kind for that matter, slurped his soup and nodded repeatedly to himself with a seeming sense of great satisfaction. Whether this response was in reaction to the situation or the soup, I would not like to hazard a guess.

"Do you think they're random?" he asked.

"Do I think what are random?"

"The string of killings, of course, Sherlock. The four murders in the Village."

"No killing is random in the true sense of the word, my dear Watson. Or, very possibly, one could say all of them are."

"I see," said Ratso, staring down intently into his matzo ball soup.

"What're you looking for?" I said. "Matzo ball leaves?"

"No, I'm just thinking, Sherlock. Do you believe the same perp committed these murders?"

"Judging merely from the proximity in time and geography, Watson, I would say there's a good chance they were done by the same hand. I haven't really looked into it."

"I have, Sherlock."

"Say what?"

"I've looked into it," said Ratso, with a not inconsiderable measure of pride. "Of course I haven't held conversations with the cops like you and McGovern and that vicious diesel dyke, Winnie Katz."

"Ah, Watson, you are blessed with such a forgiving nature. Just because she tossed you out of her lesbian dance class."

"Mad cow was named after her."

"After all, it *is* a lesbian dance class. Or at least it was a lesbian dance class. I think she's decided to take a break."

"I'd like to hire Joe the Hyena to break her legs."

"She speaks very highly of you, Watson," I said, as the waiter brought a huge corned beef sandwich for me, a huge reuben for Ratso, and a large bowl of pickles. "I'm rather in a pickle myself these days because of this singular matter of the wallet."

"That's why it's so perfect, Sherlock! What better revenge? We solve the case ourselves right under Cooperman's and Fox's noses! We've done it before! We can do it again!"

"Maybe you're on to something, Watson. You say you've been

looking into it? Marvelous! And what have you gleaned from your explorations?"

"Well, I'm sure the cops know more than they're telling us, but I have been studying the papers, the coverage on television, and the Internet."

"How ingenious of you, Watson! And you discovered precisely what, might I ask?"

"Well, for one thing, not to state the obvious, but all the victims have been men."

"Ah, Watson! Does nothing escape your scrutiny?"

"If all the vics turn out to be fags, it could be a homophobe. Or maybe a fag killing other fags."

"The hand of the killer supported by a limp wrist? I doubt it, Watson."

"There's also the fact that three of the four murder victims were divorced. That's quite a bit higher than the national average."

"Clever, Watson, clever! No detail too superficial or ridiculous for your rapacious eyes to divine! Perhaps the killer is a disgruntled marriage counselor."

"I lean to the homosexual theory."

"Don't lean too far, Watson! Don't lean too far!"

Over coffee and cheesecake, I imparted to Ratso the cutting-the-dick-off and the knitting-needle-up-the-nose tidbits. He, of course, had not heard these details before and it took him a short while to process this new and rather graphic information. Ratso habitually made the fatal, and quite irritating, mistake of thinking of everything that happened as "clues." The clues he didn't like, he ignored. The ones that appealed to him he mindlessly embraced and ruthlessly followed, like some men follow their penises around the world. It is a futile exercise and, indeed, if you take it far enough you invariably wind up fucking yourself in your own large, Jewish, slightly pear-shaped buttocks.

Yet, to paraphrase my sister Marcie, despise no thing and call no man useless. There was always something for some sad Sherlock to learn from the Watsons of the world. One of the most important things I myself had learned was never to rely on them to pick up the check.

"You may have something with this homosexual business, Watson," I remarked, as I lighted a cigar out in the street. "Perhaps we should start with me interviewing McGovern and you interviewing Winnie."

"That's fucking brilliant, Sherlock. She fucking hates my guts."

"Have I not already told you, Watson, that she speaks very highly of you? She says you have more balls than any student she's ever worked with. Of course, it *is* a lesbian dance class."

"You're serious, Sherlock?"

"I'm always serious, Watson. That's why I'm Sherlock. To paraphrase Billy Joe Shaver, I'm a serious soul nobody takes seriously."

"I take you seriously."

"That's why you're Watson," I said.

And so it was decided that the two of us would once again sally forth into that cauldron of imagined urgency that was New York to do battle with the criminal element and the powers that be. Who was behind this ugly little string of killings I had not a clue, or should I say, I had no idea. There was, in fact, only one point upon which Watson and Sherlock entirely agreed. At long last, by God, we had a case.

SIXTEEN

The next morning I met McGovern at a little breakfast place in the Village called La Bonbonniere. It was run by a charming Frenchman named Charles, who was currently the only Frenchman I knew or liked. Unless you wanted to count Victor Hugo or Joan of Arc, the latter, of course, not technically being a French-*man*, though, no doubt, she would've performed admirably in Winnie Katz's lesbian dance class had it still been in session. I had no idea what La Bonbonniere meant and I didn't really want to know. The food was good and the ambience was very basic and the café was located almost precisely midway between McGovern's place and my loft. That was why the large Irishman and I were dining there that morning. Of course, there also was the little matter of some unfinished business between us.

"Look, I'm sorry," said McGovern. "Shit happens when you're working on deadline. The guy was on a skiing vacation. He never came to your loft. We've already printed a retraction."

"Printing a retraction," I said. "That solves all the problems in the world, doesn't it?"

"Of course not," said McGovern reasonably, as he studied the menu scrutinously as if he hadn't seen it thousands of times before. "But now I think you have an even bigger problem."

"What to order?"

McGovern laughed his loud Irish laughter. Several nearby diners looked over. McGovern did not appear to notice.

"I wish that were your problem, Kink," he said at last. "I think your problem is obvious to both of us as well as the cops by now. If the murder victim was on a skiing vacation and was killed shortly after arriving back in the city, then how did his wallet get into your loft?"

"If I knew the answer to that, I wouldn't be having breakfast in a funky little café with a large, jovial Irishman."

"I'm jovial? You should tell that to my ex-wife."

"Jesus Christ, McGovern. I didn't know you were ever married."

"It was only for a week. We tried everything. Nothing worked."

I waited for McGovern to laugh, but he didn't. He just signaled the waiter and ordered two scrambled eggs, a sausage, and a croissant. I laughed inwardly—quiet, Jewish laughter. Then I ordered two eggs looking at me, like my father always used to say, and a toasted poppy-seed bagel. Oscar Wilde was right, I thought, as the waiter departed. The human soul was unknowable.

"So what are you going to do about the wallet?" asked McGovern, sipping his coffee.

"Nothing," I said. "The cops have it."

"I know that. Like Ratso would say, 'I have my sauces.'"

"What else do you know?"

"Ask specifics, Kink. The Shadow knows."

"You know about the fifth murder?"

"The one in Chelsea with the knitting needle? Where the hell do you even find a knitting needle?"

"In a knitting haystack. Do you know how victim number four was killed?"

"Yes," said McGovern, "but let's not talk about it now—the waiter's just bringing me my sausage."

"I see," I said.

And, of course, I did see. McGovern, like any good, veteran journalist in the field, knew a lot of things he didn't necessarily care to divulge. For one thing, his knowledge was the brick and mortar of his livelihood. For another, he had to always be conscious of protecting his "sauces." McGovern was also, I suspected, in somewhat of a snit because I'd expressed indifference to the investigation early on and now, admittedly, was coming back to him to try to weasel information. If I was going to get his help on this one, I'd have to play it sensitively. And sensitivity was not my long suit.

"Look, you big, obstinate fuck," I said. "Why can't we work together on this case?"

"Oh, now you want to work together on this case. Now, after I've been working my sources night and day. After you abandoned ship and went down to Texas leaving me holding the bag, or the wallet, as the case may be. Now after I've slaved for you for twenty-five years, you want to try to save our marriage."

"McGovern, I'm being rather serious here. You're having breakfast with a man who could well be the target of the NYPD's investigation. Believe me, this case is getting very close to home. I need your help."

"Those are the words I was waiting to hear," said McGovern, as he cut into his sausage. "How can I help?"

I told McGovern some of the directions in which I wanted to go with the investigation and some of the kinds of information that I would be needing. I told him that with five murders under his belt, we were already starting out under the gun, so to speak, as far as ferreting out the killer. McGovern rather pointedly asked me whose fault that was. I told him that assessing the blame should be left to God and drunks and small children, all of which—I thought but didn't mention—McGovern was capable of behaving like. Nevertheless, McGovern took it personally and said it was character assassination and I told him that if I wanted to assassinate his character I would've had to resort to nuclear weapons.

Our little brunch ended amicably enough, however, with McGovern pledging to aid the investigation in any way he could and me pumping up his balls a bit by assuring him as to how vital a role he would be playing. We'd gone through this charade many times before, it seemed, and it had always been rather tedious. The results, notwithstanding the ennui experienced in gaining them, had been indisputable. Like it or not, McGovern and I were a team.

"I'll be in touch with you, Watson," I told him as I left the place.

"That's what I'm afraid of," he said.

I went back to my empty loft and my empty life, but at least now I had something to do with my mind. To paraphrase Sherlock, the man is nothing, the work is all. Everybody in New York had a project and I was no exception to the rule. I would catch this killer who had already taken five lives. That was my project. It made for a rather cold, loveless hobby, but as a project, it was passionate.

I called Rambam and, as fate would have it, I reached him on his shoe phone. As fate would also have it, he was in the neighborhood. This was good because I didn't really know where in the hell to start on the case, and on the personal side, I was only a few steps away from attempting to commit suicide by jumping through a ceiling fan. This was bad because I needed all the fans I could get.

"I'll be right over," he said. "I always enjoy hanging out with people who are targets of murder investigations."

"Thanks, pal," I told him.

It was a sunny, cold day outside. Inside the loft it seemed dark and numb and threatening, something you could only guess at by the way it felt in your bones. I sat down at the desk, lit a cigar, and looked to Sherlock for answers. He didn't have any. Neither did I. I was losing my hair and losing my mind and losing what little faith I had left in my fellow man. I'm losing, said Frank Sinatra just before he died. I'm losing, too, I thought. And the funny thing was I didn't really give a shit. By the time Rambam showed up, it was ten minutes too late to make any difference.

"Fuck!" said Rambam. "This place not only feels like a tomb, it's as cold as a tomb."

"I didn't notice."

"Jesus! There's no sign of life!"

"Oh, please. Just sit down."

"I mean, the cat's gone."

"Brilliant! What else do your powers of observation tell you?"

"I don't even hear the lesbian dance class pounding away up there."

"Winnie's giving the class a break. She's spending her free time collaborating with the cops."

"Never trust a lesbian."

"You can say that again."

"Never trust a lesbian."

I looked at Rambam sitting across the desk from me in the client's chair that seemed to have been so empty for so long. There was no question this was the kind of case any private investigator would give his pebbled glass to sink his teeth into. The killer, clearly a psycho, was at least imaginative. Rambam looked handsome and clean-cut and efficient. He looked like a thinking man's Archie Goodwin. And if he was Archie Goodwin, then I must be Nero Wolfe. Sherlock was thin and Wolfe was fat, and the only qualities they shared were a passion for the truth and the fact that they both were very lonely men.

"Okay, Archie," I said. "Report."

"You've got to be kidding."

"Archie Goodwin was a great investigator. He was Nero Wolfe's eyes, legs, and sometimes, his heart."

"I'm probably the only one of your friends who even knows who Archie Goodwin was."

"That's why you're him."

"You really have gone around the bend, you know."

"Archie! Report!"

"Okay, Mr. Wolfe, here we go. We don't have shit. How's that? We have to rely on your drinking buddy McGovern and the cops for our information, and the cops aren't sharing. So, in short, Mr. Wolfe, we're fucked."

"Hardly, Archie. You know as well as I that we're far from fucked. Perhaps you are merely being slothful and indolent. There have been a myriad of cases that the NYPD has failed to solve that subsequently have evolved into metaphysical notches on our belt."

"And that's a hell of a big belt."

"Stop mumbling, Archie. I can't hear you."

"This is insane," said Rambam, laughing to himself in a danger-ous-sounding way and looking at me with unbridled pity in his eyes. "As you've said on many occasions, Mr. Wolfe, the cops have all the manpower and all the resources and we can't compete with them in those areas."

"'Areae' is the Latin plural."

"What we need to do, not to mention a few sit-ups on your part, is to approach this case from an angle the cops may have ignored. Maybe tackle it from behind."

"You're not suggesting anal sex?"

"All I'm saying, you sick, sedentary bastard, is that I'm going to crank up the ol' hard-boiled computer and then we'll see what it has to say about the backgrounds of the five victims. The cops have been over this ground already, of course, but there's always something you miss on the first go around. I'm sure a man of your genius will be able to pick up on the details they've missed. You may actually have to leave the brownstone for some of this. I may need some backup."

"Are you suggesting anal sex?"

"I'm suggesting you better go upstairs and water your tulips before I punch you in the nose."

"Orchids, Archie. Not tulips. Tulips are so pedestrian. I think I will go upstairs and water my orchids."

"I'll warn Winnie."

"Maybe I'll just ring for some beer. Thank you, Archie. You're dismissed."

"Hell," said Rambam, as he goose-stepped toward the door. "It's almost enough to make you miss Sherlock."

"Right you are, Watson," I said.

"*Almost* enough," he said.

SEVENTEEN

I once asked the famed Texas defense lawyer, Racehorse Haynes, if he would be willing to do some pro bono work on a case with which I was involved. Before Racehorse could answer, our mutual friend and brilliant lawyer David Berg piped up: "The words 'Racehorse' and 'pro bono' are never used in the same sentence."

That was kind of how it was with Rambam. I was aware, of course, that Rambam had a right to earn a living. Though the work he'd done for and with me paid very well in the coin of the spirit, it was never going to help him pay the rent. The problem was that Rambam's other work tended to be of a global nature, taking him suddenly off to solve the strange matter of *The Giant Rat of Lower Baboon's Asshole* at almost precisely the moment I needed him most right here in little old New York City. I never begrudged Rambam for taking a paying gig, but as a friend and fellow investigator, the timing of his travels did tend to irk me. It seemed ungracious to complain too much, however, especially considering how many times he'd actually laid his life on the line for the Kinkster.

Thus, it was not surprising when, several days later, I met Rambam in Chinatown and he informed me that he had good news and bad news. We were at a new place of Rambam's choosing, and the beef chow fun with black bean sauce and the salt and pepper shrimp were definitely killer bee. Big Wong's still took top awards for the soup, however. A bowl of won ton mein at Big Wong's could cure almost all the ills of the world. *Almost* all the ills of the world. It was another cold, dreary afternoon in the city and the moods of its occupants paralleled the weather fairly closely. Rambam seemed, however, in what for him was a rather cheerful, almost chirpy frame of mind. By trained deductive reasoning I concluded that he'd soon be traveling to sunnier climes. This, I suspected, was the bad news. As to the good news, I didn't have a clue.

"This fucking place has Big Wong's beat hands down," said Rambam, as he went to work on a whole steamed flounder that took up nearly half the table.

"You're just mad because a waiter there splashed hot tea on you. That's how they wash the tables. They splash hot tea on them. It's one of the colorful traditions I like at Big Wong's. You just made the mistake of sitting down before they'd finished cleaning the table."

"One mistake I won't make is going back there again."

There was a certain ethnic trait in Rambam that kept him from discussing what was clearly on both of our minds until the food had arrived and largely been consumed. Maybe he just liked to keep his cards close to his lobster bib. At any rate, Rambam finally decided to bring the annual meeting of the Brotherhood of the Flaming Asshole to order. He was brief with his opening remarks.

"Do you want the good news first," he asked, "or the bad news?"

"I'm Jewish," I said. "I'll take the bad news first."

"I'm leaving tomorrow for Cambodia. I'd hoped I could postpone it but I can't. This is an urgent, not to mention very lucrative, case."

Rambam traveled the globe on a fairly regular basis, and he was also given to leaving at short notice, so the only thing that surprised me was how little the news really surprised me. I took it in rather stoically.

"Give my regards to Angkor Wat."

"Wat?" shouted Rambam. "Can't hear you. I got a chopstick in my ear."

"Okay," I said, "what's the good news?"

"The good news is that the hard-boiled computer didn't let us down. I fed the names of the five victims into it and it clearly affirmed that three of the five were scumbags."

"That *is* a hard-boiled computer."

"The point is, even in New York, three out of five victims turning out to be scumbags is, to say the least, statistically improbable."

"Define 'scumbag.'"

"For our purposes it would comprise individuals with rap sheets full of abuse toward women. I'm talking rape, forced sodomy, every manner of domestic violence you can imagine. Now, remember, that's only three of the stiffs. The other two, for the moment, seem to come up clean. But, believe me, it's suggestive. Very fucking suggestive."

"Very fucking suggestive of what?"

"How the fuck should I know? Archie Goodwin's blowing out for Cambodia tomorrow at three o'clock and I haven't even packed my pith helmet yet. It's up to you, Mr. Wolfe. You and Ratso, your favorite Dr. Watson."

"Aren't you mixing metaphors a bit? If only for balance, you need a skinny guy and a fat guy, and Wolfe and Watson are too endomorphically similar. So I'll be Sherlock and Ratso will be Watson."

"Boy, if the killer could hear that, I bet he'd be quaking in his boots."

It did sound pretty ridiculous, I reflected, as I scooped up the last salt and pepper shrimp just ahead of Rambam's rapacious hand.

What the hell did it matter anyway? The whole thing was going to be ten times as hard with Rambam out of the picture. It was true that Ratso and I had solved more than a few high-profile cases on our own, but this time the perpetrator was clearly a serial psycho suffering from an overactive imagination. Times like these required every hand on board, and the whole team working together, not to mix a metaphor. And this was modern-day New York, not Victorian London. The Sherlock-Watson business might be an effective therapeutic game for Ratso—hell, even possibly for myself—but deductive reasoning doesn't always fare so well when pitted against brutal, violent, twisted, miscreative, undecaffeinated evil. Even with Rambam, this one looked like a bitch from hell.

"Where do you think we should start?" I asked.

"You start with the two murder victims whose backgrounds appear to be clean. Right now we just have an unusual statistical circumstance. For there to be a pattern, there has to be a pattern. Capisce?"

"I think so."

"Look, if these two supposedly clean guys are really clean, then this particular statistical universe might as well circle the bowl. If you and your pet rodent can't dig up something on those two guys, then whatever you have on the other three is probably irrelevant. There's a reason somebody systematically whacks five people. It may not be especially logical. It may not be apparent on the surface. But, trust me, it's there. These are not Son of Sam affairs or random thrill killings. There's method in this guy's madness."

"There's also madness in his method," I said.

"No shit, Sherlock," said Rambam grimly. "Don't fucking get careless."

Before we parted company that afternoon Rambam reached into the inside pocket of his jacket and handed me an envelope that he said contained everything the hard-boiled computer had spit out regarding the case. The envelope did not seem terribly thick. Maybe the hard-boiled computer had other things on its mind. I told Rambam as much. I also told him I thought that all computers were the work of Satan. No, he said, the work of Satan was what Ratso and I would soon be investigating.

Eventually, Rambam went back to that faraway kingdom called Brooklyn, and I walked home alone. Along the way, a refrain from a Billy Joe Shaver song, "Freedom's Child," kept running through my head. "Fillin' up the empty space, left by one who's gone." The problem was that there were getting to be so many empty spaces in my life that pretty soon I was going to need a fucking backhoe.

EIGHTEEN

I thought I heard Rambam's plane flying over my head some time that morning, but it could have been a garbage truck. For all I knew it could've been a nuclear missile coming to turn my eyes to jelly. I'd stayed up late the previous night with a bottle of Jameson's, poring over the rather skimpy results the hard-boiled computer had—rather grudgingly, it seemed to me—spit out. Rambam had told me quite clearly that the hard-boiled computer was at heart merely a rather extensive criminal database that very easily could miss important, even seminal, information just as the cops often did. It ain't the Bible, Rambam had said. What was it then? I asked. Think of it as a roadmap to hell, Rambam had answered. I didn't mention it to Rambam at the time, but why would you need a roadmap if you were already there?

Bright and early that morning, around noon, I called Ratso and was rewarded by hearing his loud, rodentlike voice go through my head like a drill bit. We decided to go over the printouts together and Ratso, who seemed to have become more insular as the years had gone by, was able to persuade me to make my annual pilgrimage to his apartment. He would make tea if I would bring some pastries up from the place across the street. Ratso's apartment would not be the most pleasant garden spot in which to have tea and pastries, but logistically, it did make some sense. One of the two killings in question had taken place in SoHo, only blocks from where he lived on Prince Street.

The sun was peeping out between the clouds and the buildings as I ankled it over to Ratso's that afternoon, and I had to admit it was bordering on a beautiful day, with all the taxis and pigeons and people milling about like wayward stars in a pleasantly fucked-up universe. Walking's always a good mode of transport because it clears the mind and sometimes you can even think. I was thinking that it was possible that things weren't as bad as maybe they'd seemed to be in the recent past. Okay, the cat was gone. There was nothing I could do about that until I crossed the rainbow bridge and met up with her again. But other than that, I was still a free bird, and my pattern of flight was taking me right where I loved to be, into the dark heart of a murder investigation. Happiness, it appeared, really was a warm gun.

It felt, to paraphrase my father, almost good to be alive. Now if Ratso and I could just poke around a bit and find a few blemishes on the backgrounds of the two "clean" victims, we might really get somewhere with this affair. From the very nature of the murders that I was aware of, I could already deduce an avenging angel perpetrating the crimes. Possibly the relative or brother or boyfriend of one of the sexual abuse victims. That would make a lot of sense, always provided the two backgrounds didn't remain clean after Ratso and I got through with them. Hell, I thought, nothing remained clean after Ratso got through with it.

His apartment, I soon discovered, not to my enormous surprise, also fell into this category. Coke cans and old pizza cartons littered the coffee table, and about forty-nine hockey sticks that had apparently been leaned precariously against the doorjamb crashed into my cigar as it entered Ratso's rather fetid airspace. Ratso came out of his lair still wearing his pajamas, which were bright green with dollar signs all over them. I didn't get to comment on his apparel, however, because I was still trying to extricate myself from all the hockey sticks.

"Great!" he shouted enthusiastically. "My alarm still works."

"You could've just locked the door," I said, not irrationally.

"Oh, I do. I always keep it triple-locked because I've got a lifetime of stuff in here. But when I buzzed you in, I had to take a sudden dump, so I just left the door unlocked for the time it took you to come up in the elevator, then went to take the dump, and you can see the results. Not of the dump, I mean, of your attempted entry into the apartment. What do you think, Sherlock?"

"Very ingenious, Watson, very ingenious! Now if I can remove the hockey stick that's embedded in my scrotum, maybe I can come into your fucking apartment."

Once you got past the clutter, browsing Ratso's little apartment could be quite an educational experience, especially if your areas of interest were pornography, Jesus Christ, Bob Dylan, or Hitler. At the moment, indeed, a fairly salacious porno tape was running on one of Ratso's many television sets, the sound thankfully muted. A life-size statue of the Virgin Mary looked on in stoic silence as well. On the kitchen counter, along with leftover takeout Chinese food that had to have been there at least several fortnights, there stood a large wicker basket of little black puppetheads, the brothers and sisters of the one currently residing on my mantel at 199B Vandam Street. The way the basket was so prominently positioned, its contents might have been apples for people from Mars. Of course, not that many earthlings ever came into Ratso's chambers either. I suspect he believed that too much traffic might be a security risk. And then there were the books—shelves and shelves containing every angle and aspect of the lives of Hitler, Jesus, and Bob Dylan. What, I wondered, did the three have in common? Possibly only that Larry "Ratso" Sloman devotedly collected them.

"I see the maid hasn't come this week," I said, my eye falling upon Ratso's old disreputable couch with the skidmarks on it. "Or did you kill her and take her to your Lord?"

"She came all right," said Ratso, with a measure of pride. "Right there on the couch."

It was hard for me to believe that I'd once called that same decrepit, soiled sofa home. It was even harder to believe that Ratso was the man the fates had chosen to be my Dr. Watson. Nevertheless, he had many good qualities, almost none of which sprang to mind as I looked at him standing in the middle of his sick, debauched little apartment in his green pajamas with the dollar signs. Call no man useless, I thought.

"Let's get down to business, Sherlock," he said at last. "Where are the pastries?"

After a very civilized tea and pastry continental brunch in Ratso's squalid quarters, I had revised upward my rough calculation of the man's worth to the investigation. Not only was he perhaps a little too familiar with the living street, he knew someone who lived in the same building in which one of the two murders had occurred. For a private investigator, especially an amateur like myself, this was a bird's nest on the ground. The cops could waltz right in any time they desired, but even the licensed PI has difficulty interviewing friends, neighbors, and relatives of stiffs.

Call no man useless, I reflected, as Ratso and I marched up Prince Street, headed toward the recent scene of the crime. Apartments turn over fast in New York and the murder had taken place over a week ago, so it was entirely possible that this could be a wipeout even with Ratso's contact in the building. By now the victim's place could have been sanitized, painted, and inhabited by anyone from a large, extended Pakistani family to Will and Grace.

"What's your friend's name again?" I asked, as we continued up the sidewalk.

"Harry Felcher. He's a performance artist."

"Don't you think we ought to call him and make sure he's home?"

"He's a nocturnal creature. Always home in the daytime. He's a bit like you, Sherlock. Maybe a bit more eccentric."

"That's impossible, Watson."

"Not really. He started out as a female impersonator, but he seems lately to have overidentified with his field of study. Now he actually believes he's Nina Simone or Billie Holiday."

"So he's black?"

"No. He's white as Peruvian marching powder."

"Bit of a stretch, isn't it, Watson? How does he get past not being black?"

"Same way he gets past not having a vagina," said Ratso, as he hooked a left at the corner.

The building itself looked like the kind of structure in which a murder might have taken place recently. I checked the address against Rambam's printout. This was the place, all right. But you would've known that even without the printout. All you needed was a measure of native sensitivity. It was like looking at the eyes of a person in a photograph that you knew to be dead.

"I'll buzz Harry, Sherlock," said Ratso, as he headed across the street.

"Fine, Watson, fine."

In a matter of moments we were buzzed in and were riding up to the fourth floor in a small elevator that smelled better than the one in Ratso's building. Cuban cigar smoke, of course, improves anything. Harry Felcher met us at the elevator. He was wearing a bright pink kimono and a lot of lipstick and makeup. He looked like a dead diva, which was not that far off the mark, as he immediately treated us to a few verses of "Over the Rainbow" while he escorted us to his boudoir.

If anything, the place was weirder than Harry. It looked like a miniature neon jungle, with mannequins, wigs, high-heeled stilettos, lingerie of every type imaginable—everything a nice Jewish boy from New York needed in his apartment. Old-time, rather spooky ballroom music was playing on an actual Victrola. Everything smelled like stale perfume.

"Nice place," said Ratso.

"We like it," said Felcher.

Who the "we" was was not entirely clear, since there was no sign of anyone else inhabiting the small apartment. Ratso, possessing fewer social graces than myself, was the first to voice the question.

"We?" he said.

"Me and Judy," said Felcher.

There was an uncomfortable silence in the place for a moment or two. This was broken by Felcher, who began dancing around and singing, "If tiny little bluebirds fly ov-er the rainbow, why, oh, why can't I?" Ratso and I dutifully gave him a light round of applause. Then it was half-past time to get down to business.

"There was a murder in this building last week," said Ratso. "Did you know the vic?"

"The vic?" asked Felcher.

"The vic-tim," said Ratso irritably. "Don Rossetti?"

"I knew Don and his wife, Celeste," said Felcher, eerily maintaining his Judy Garland voice and mannerisms as he spoke.

"Any idea who murdered him?" Ratso asked.

"No, no Nanette!" Felcher ejaculated. "I don't like to think about things like that."

"No one likes to think about things like that," said Ratso, a bit more patiently. "Except for Sherlock here, of course."

"Fine, Watson, fine," I muttered.

Now it truly was a ship of fools, I thought. Here were Ratso and I, playing at being Sherlock Holmes and Dr. Watson, interviewing this Harry Felcher person, who was, to put it kindly, playing at being Judy Garland. Maybe none of us were playing at all. Maybe this was life and life only. Maybe the only thing that was real was the guy who had died in this building.

"Rossetti's name isn't on the buzzer," said Ratso. "Do you know where they lived in the building?"

"But, of course," said Felcher, with a highly theatrical wave of his arm. "Right down the hall."

"Tell us everything you know about them," said Ratso. "This is important, Judy. I mean, Harry."

"I answer to both," gushed Felcher. "Okay, let me see. They were a strange couple. She was a dancer, and like all dancers she was a klutz. She was always breaking a finger or an arm or falling down the stairs and getting a concussion."

Ratso looked at me knowingly at this point. Felcher, of course, in his total self-absorption, did not notice. He kept rattling on, which was fine with me. I've always enjoyed hearing Judy Garland impersonators speak the truth, as they know it, to a world unwilling to be led to the light.

"Don was always a quiet sort of brooding fellow. Never said much, yet there was something about him that made you feel uncomfortable in his presence. Celeste, though, she was an angel. She left a few weeks before it happened. I don't know why she left. She's back, by the way, cleaning out the apartment. At least that's what I think she said."

This time Ratso and I looked at each other. Just down the hall, apparently, was the woman whom the hard-boiled computer might very well have missed, which meant the cops might very well have missed her as well. Don Rossetti's clean reputation might be about to be getting a wee bit dirtier. But it was still all conjecture. When you're standing in the apartment of a full-tilt Judy Garland impersonator, the whole world is, indubitably, conjecture.

"If tiny little bluebirds fly—" Felcher began again. But this time Ratso cut him off rather abruptly.

"Hold it, Judy!" he said, gently but firmly. "Celeste is in the dead man's apartment right now?"

"It's number-4C-to-the-right," sang Judy, hewing tightly to the melody line.

Then she finished with a flourish, pirouetting passionately about the small, cluttered, fetish-fraught living room. Ratso and I stood stolidly by and watched with the eyes of men who were witnessing the wreck of a toy train.

"Why—oh—why—can't—I?" she sang, in an almost uncanny imitation of the real thing. Maybe it was as close to the real thing as either one of us was ever going to get.

"I think we have what we need, Watson," I said.

NINETEEN

Celeste Rossetti was not only in, we discovered, she was also very open and forthcoming regarding her estranged husband, who, of course, was now even further estranged since he was dead. She had been visiting relatives out of state, she said, so she had not yet talked with the cops. At this disclosure, Ratso gave me a long, meaningful glance, almost like a lover. This irritated me, quite understandably, because he was telegraphing shit to the interviewee that could derail the process faster than God makes Wal-Marts. I ignored Ratso and tried to focus on Celeste. She was an attractive and bright woman and, to my mind, a good candidate for an abusive relationship. It did not take her long to confirm my suspicions.

Don Rossetti had been sweet as pie during their courtship, but after the marriage, he lost his job with the city, and things seemed to sour from there. That's when the dark side of her husband began to emerge.

"I hear you're a dancer," Ratso piped in at one point. "What kind of dancer?"

"I love all kinds of dance," she said. "I'm not dancing much these days, after the marriage and this nightmare of what happened to

Don. But I'll get back to it. I used to do some really modern, experimental things."

"Ever heard of Winnie Katz?" Ratso persisted.

"I don't believe it!" cried Celeste. "I took her classes for a while."

"So did I," said Ratso.

"Don stepped in, of course, and made me stop," said Celeste ruefully.

"The same thing happened to me," said Ratso.

"Your husband made you stop going?" Celeste asked Ratso, winking broadly at me.

"No," said Ratso, with an edge of lingering bitterness. "Winnie threw me out."

I have long had a little amateur private investigator theory that actresses, models, singers, performers, and dancers, especially dancers, tend to be magnets for abusive men. Whether it is that they seek direction or that they take it so well, I'm not certain. But Judy Garland's description of Celeste's injuries and the fact that she was a dancer and the fact that her husband had been croaked along with three certified abusers was enough for me to get right to the meat of it.

"Was your husband physically abusive to you, Celeste?" I asked, not unkindly.

"God, yes!" she responded immediately. "And then some."

Ratso was now smiling broadly, a reaction totally inappropriate to the proceedings at hand. What you saw was what you got with Ratso, of course. He was the perfect Dr. Watson, totally devoid of duplicity. I would have to talk to him about keeping a bit more of a poker-face in future, however.

"What did you do?" I asked.

"I thought about going to the police, but I ran into a shrink at the health food store. A very nice and understanding man named Dr. Goldfine. I began seeing him and then I began seeing him, if you get my drift. And now, as soon as I close this place up, I'll be moving in with him."

Ratso now looked on with an expression that could only be called a leer. It was, of course, somewhat unprofessional for a shrink to be hosing one of his patients, but, I suppose, it happened all the time. Sometimes even a private investigator got lucky.

"Well," I said, "I think that's about all we'll be needing. You have no idea who might've killed your husband?"

"None," she said lightly, as she began stacking dishes into a cardboard box.

"Then we wish you and Dr. Goldfine all the best for the future," I said.

"Thanks," she said. "We're going on a cruise to Hawaii next week."

"I think we have all we need, Watson," I said.

TWENTY

I n a sense, we were just doing legwork, picking up pieces of the puzzle that the cops and the hard-boiled computer might have missed. Realistically, we were not much closer to solving the case or identifying the killer than we had been before, but there was a certain degree of promise that had presented itself. If the cops had missed Celeste, what else might they have overlooked? The NYPD had the means and the manpower, all right, but they were far from infallible. I was fairly sure by now that the abusive husband or boyfriend angle would hold up with the fifth murder victim as, indeed, it had with the other four. Five out of five would undeniably provide a motive for this maniacal murder spree. And a motive was as good a place to start as any.

I decided not to lecture Ratso on his bedside manner during interviews. He was pumped about the success of the Celeste Rossetti visit, and, to be perfectly candid, I was a little surprised as well at how easily it had all come to pass. We didn't really have to check out the scene of the one remaining victim, but I figured we were on a roll. This was the most recent victim, the guy in Chelsea that the cops had found with a knitting needle rammed up his nose and into his brain.

There was no doubt in my mind that we would find something dark and sinister lurking in this victim's background. But as things transpired, even I was a bit blindsided by what we were soon to discover.

It was late afternoon by the time we got down to Chelsea, with Ratso very much wanting to stop for a lunch break in Chinatown. I told him we'd make quick work of the fifth guy's crime scene, provided we could even get into the building. Then we'd go to Chinatown and plot our next amusement. This building looked very similar to all the others on the street. You wouldn't have thought that less than a week had gone by since a guy had had a knitting needle jammed into his head on these very premises. But sometimes, in little, almost undetectable ways, the crime stays with the scene.

We were in luck with this one as well. The guy's name was right there on the buzzer: Jordan Skelton. 6E. We didn't know if anyone would be answering, of course. Could be new occupants already. Could be the ghost of a man with a knitting needle in his medulla oblongata. Could be nobody home. You roll the dice and you play it as it lays. I pushed the buzzer. Nothing happened. I pushed it again. We waited a few moments and I pushed it a third time. Nothing. So I pushed all the buzzers in the building. A moment later, the door buzzed open.

We ankled it into the lobby only to discover that the building's one elevator was out of order. So Ratso and I legged it up to the sixth floor by which time we began to truly understand from whence the term "legwork" had derived. Perhaps, I thought, we should've called this one in from the deli. On the other hand, a good little private investigator leaves no detail unexplored, no witness uninterviewed, no road untaken. Sometimes you pursue the investigation; sometimes the investigation appears to pursue you. Either circumstance, of course, can often be extremely tedious.

Finding Jordan Skelton's previous place of residence was no problem. We walked down the deserted hallway to 6E. No signs of activity. No police crime scene gift-wrappings. We knocked on the door. No sounds from within the apartment. No one answered the door. No sounds in the hallway at all, actually, except Ratso carping in my ear about *now* going to Chinatown. That could well have been the end of it, no doubt, but the Lord commanded me to persist in my knocking upon just another one of heaven's doors. I listened again, more closely this time, and I knew I'd either been blessed or cursed by the ancient God of the Hebrews. Time would tell, of course. In the meantime, I could definitely hear muffled sounds within the apartment.

"Yes?" said a tentative female voice. "Who is it?"

"It's Richard and Larry," I said. "Friends of Jordan. Just wanted to come by and see if there was anything we could do. Can we come in?"

The sounds of a chain being removed from a door. The door opens. A grieving, ghostly, strawberry blonde puts her beautiful head into the hallway. No makeup. Nothing left but guts and glory.

"I didn't know Jordan had any friends," she said.

"Boys' club," I said. "He probably wouldn't have mentioned it."

"You know," Ratso interjected, "hockey, poker, pickup basketball games, occasional bowling nights?"

"That doesn't sound like Jordan," she said. I felt like shoving a knitting needle into Ratso's brain.

"Sometimes we don't know everything about even the people we think we know best," I said. "What's your name?"

"Heather," she said, leaving the door open for us to follow her back into the room. "Heather Lay."

She walked with shapely grace, a trim little figure, like a bird imbued with the God-given certainty that it could fly safely through the storm. We followed her into the living room and sat down on the sofa.

"You're the only visitors I've had since the police were here," she said, stating simple fact. "So make yourselves comfortable."

So the cops had interviewed her, apparently, and Jordan Skelton's background was still a question mark at best, at least as far as the hard-boiled computer was concerned. Heather Lay was smart, you could tell that. Smart and brave and strong. I found myself admiring what I saw as her ability to embody Churchill's credo: "When you're going through hell, keep going." But, no doubt, it's easier said than done.

"I'll tell you what I'm going to do," said Heather. "I'm going to make us all some tea."

"Don't bother," I said. "We just—"

"It's no trouble," she said. "In fact, I think I'd like to do it. You both seem very nice. And I'd like to hear about Jordan."

Ratso rolled his eyes almost in sight of the woman and when she went into the kitchen he made a vaguely masturbatory gesture with his hand. I had to agree that this could present a bit of a problem. Should we level with the poor woman, I wondered, and risk losing her confidence? Or should we simply continue to fake it, after the fashion that most of us have followed for most of our adult lives? Honesty may be the best policy, but when in doubt, always fake it, and that's exactly what we planned to do. Get Heather to talk about Jordan and, we hoped, she wouldn't notice that we wouldn't have known the guy if we'd stepped on him—which was no longer possible, of course, because he was six feet under. That was the plan, anyway, and it almost worked.

Things rocked along for the next ten minutes or so, with Heather coming in and out of the kitchen, still remarking on the things she never knew about Jordan, and Ratso, warming to the new role as Jordan's friend, tossing out little crumbs to the grieving girlfriend. Finally, he seemed to be getting so dangerously out on a limb that I felt it was time to intercede. I pointed out the fact that just as there were many things Heather didn't know about her late boyfriend, there were probably a few things Larry and Richard didn't know about him as well. Maybe she could tell us about the other side of Jordan Skelton? This, I hoped, would have the dual effect of getting Ratso to pull his lips together and prodding Heather to open up.

"Jordan was always being misunderstood," she said. "He really was a genius, but he was always getting fired from jobs. He worked so hard, but his bosses never appreciated it. He tried everything, poor baby. Nobody ever gave him a real chance. His family didn't. His former wife didn't. He thought everybody was against him. He just never had any luck. He tried so hard, poor baby."

It has long been my theory that women who use the phrase "poor baby" about their men don't really know their men very well. Also, Heather was reciting her lines about the dearly departed almost like a Stepford wife. She had to know better. When she brought me a cup of tea I got a good close look at the face of an angel. Her eyes seemed to be waiting to sparkle. Yet her words had been those of the typical abused woman in denial about the true nature of her man. She was smart, soulful, beautiful, and every native instinct I had in stock told me she'd been knocked around pretty badly by this guy. Why did scumbags, to borrow a common term of Rambam's, so often seem to wind up with wonderful women like Heather? I wondered. Was it just something in the nature of woman? Or was it just something in the nature of man?

"But back to your questions about Jordan's 'other side'—hell, I don't know," said Heather ruefully, as we all sipped at our tea. "I've been trying to pull my head out of my ass for two years now, so the truth is, I don't know which side was up."

The remark certainly brought the tea party to attention. To me it indicated a toughness and awareness in Heather that she'd no doubt had to park at the door for much of her relationship with the scumbag. Yet it was those very qualities that had kept her from becoming a totally broken woman, that would soon, hopefully, help her mend and get on with her life.

"I take this to mean," I said, "that he did cause you physical harm?"

Heather, whom I now observed had beautiful freckles, fixed me with a look that somehow managed to make eye contact with my soul. She was clearly, and not unpleasantly, I thought, taking the measure of the man. The man, of course, being me. It felt surprisingly good to be focused upon by Heather. How could a woman like this ever fall for such a scumbag?

"I take that to mean," she said, "that you weren't really Jordan's friends?"

"No," I said, for once not having to fake sincerity. "We're *your* friends."

I don't remember the small talk, if any, that occurred after that. She collected the tea cups and saucers like a little girl playing house. At some point I gave her my card, stopping just short, I believe, of begging her to call me. At the door, she started to shake hands, then ended up hugging both of us, an unexpected move that surprised Ratso, and surprised me even more because it almost brought a tear to my eye.

As we headed down the mountain of stairwells, farther and farther from Heather Lay, Ratso and I did not speak. Neither of us, in fact, said a word until we were out on the street. All the way down, we had been in our own little worlds, as if leaving a synagogue or church after a wedding, or a bone orchard after a funeral. For all I knew, Ratso had been reflecting upon Chinatown. For my part, I had been reflecting upon what it might take to put the sparkle back in Heather Lay's eyes.

"Do you think she'll call?" Ratso said at last.

"I doubt it," I said. "Too proud."

"What I want to know," said Ratso, "is how a woman that proud could let herself become abused?"

"The same way," I said, "that a brave man can let himself become afraid."

TWENTY-ONE

The days went by like gypsy moths; the nights like lazy fireflies. There was a measure of easement in my soul and I attributed that to having met Heather Lay. Not that I ever expected to see her or her glorious freckles again, but merely the knowledge that someone like her was in this world, waiting atop six flights of stairs and a broken elevator, seemed to give my crazy existence all the affirmation it needed. Now I was not just burning the candle at both its ends; now in the waxy countenance of that imaginary candle there was something I'd never really seen before: a flicker of hope.

I felt with some certitude that Heather, though she didn't cop to it in so many words, was an abused woman. She had seemed to me like a diamond in the rough, and the rough, I suspected, had really been rough. Maybe what I saw in her was the raw, noble humanity that was left after everything else had been stripped away. As Oscar Wilde had said, "What fire doesn't destroy, it hardens." And yet, she wasn't hard. She was a woman who had flowered into a beautiful, doomed bloom of what Nelson Algren had called "achieved innocence." Not the innocence a baby is born with, or a young child often naturally possesses, but the innocence of a woman who's probably had the shit beaten out of her many times, not to mention the more subtle and often more deadly soul-grinding experiences that are endemic in an abusive relationship. The courageous innocence of a woman who's lost a bad man she loved, and must continue to go on living. And if Heather could do it, after all the heartaches and disappointments and tragedies that life had sent her way—if Heather could do it, so could I.

So throw another Jew on the fire. Warm your hands replete with the broken fingers of life. When all the innocence you were born with is gone, what is left, my friend, is always worth keeping.

Hell, I thought, as I sipped a hot espresso one morning in the brittle sunlight that slanted in from the kitchen window, I wish the cat were here to talk to. What a great conversationalist she was! Never argued. Never really listened except with her heart. Never pretended to be interested when she wasn't. Never said a fucking thing. People could learn a lot from cats. They could probably learn a lot from dung beetles, too. If you thought about it, we were all novices at life, and we rarely became more experienced with experience. Or maybe we do become more experienced, but we rarely become more wise. I was wise enough, however, to finally realize that the cat was in a better place. Whether it was some distant garbage can or across the rainbow bridge, I knew she'd landed on her feet. Now it was my turn to do the same.

I plucked an Epicure Number 2 out of Sherlock's head, lopped the butt off with a facileness wrought by years of practice, and prepared for ignition. Striking a kitchen match deftly upon my strides, I fired her up. Hell, I was so good at it I could've done it in my sleep if it weren't for the obvious fire hazard. I leaned back in the chair and started to blow the smoke up toward the lesbian dance class until I realized that it wasn't there. Fuck me dead, mate. There were a lot of things that weren't there anymore. The years had gone by like young women sliding over my face.

This was the nature of the worldly and unworldly thoughts I was thinking when I was interrupted by the ringing of the two red telephones. I took a few existential puffs on the cigar, then collared the blower on the left.

"Start talkin'," I said.

"MIT! MIT! MIT!"

"To whom am I speaking?"

Obviously, it was McGovern. Obviously, there was a problem of some sort. I took another patient puff on my cigar.

"Are you sitting down?" he asked.

"No. I'm hanging upside-down from my inversion table. What's so fucking important?"

"I just thought you'd like to know that the killer's confessed."

TWENTY-TWO

McGovern had a little more but not much. His sources at the cop shop said they definitely had the killer in custody. The guy had signed a written confession and the cops were convinced they had their boy, although McGovern didn't as yet know his name. But in the Village, once the news hit, there would be a long, collective sigh of relief. This, of course, was understandable, if somewhat premature. It is a rather widespread misconception that innocent people do not confess to crimes they didn't commit. This notion is flat wrong. False confession is rooted in the very nature of man. For instance, more than two hundred people confessed to the kidnapping of the Lindbergh baby. The cops had more than thirty signed, written confessions in the famous case of the Black Dahlia murder in Los Angeles in the late forties. In that case, the murder and dismemberment of actress Elizabeth Short, the real killer is still unknown. Then there is the well-documented time the cowardly kraut Himmler thought that he'd lost his favorite pipe. He eventually found it on the seat of his truck where he'd left it, but in the interval, six concentration camp inmates had signed written confessions that they'd stolen it. When I meet Himmler in hell I'm going to take his fucking pipe and shove it up his ass. At any rate, because of interrogation techniques, the desire to see that fucking smile of acceptance on that fucking face of that fucking cop, the ambition of having our fifteen minutes of shame, or the fact that many of us just don't give a damn whether we live or die anymore just as long as we get a good table in a restaurant, an ungodly large number of false confessions have come into being. DNA tests are proving every day that this is true.

I am not a Catholic priest; I don't believe in confessions. Like Sherlock Holmes, all I believe in is the irrefutable, undeniable, unforgivable evidence. I walked over to the huge, gleaming espresso machine, drew another cup of hot, bitter espresso, and accompanied it back to the desk. I was kind of in a hot, bitter mood myself. I thought of my own firsthand encounter with Max Soffar, who's been in solitary confinement for twenty-three years on death row in Texas. It is mute commentary to what a confession can do when tossed into the well-oiled workings of a broken system. It is a reminder that the lowest form of society is not the criminal class. The lowest form of society are those who guard the criminal class. What follows are a few actual pages from the Kinkster's casebook.

I'd never interviewed anyone on death row until one January when I picked up a telephone and looked through a clear plastic divider at the haunting reflection of my own humanity in the eyes of Max Soffar. Max doesn't have a lot of time and neither do I, so I'll try to keep this brief and to the point. "I'm not a murderer," he told me. "I want people to know that I'm not a murderer. That means more to me than anything. It means more to me than freedom."

Somewhere along the line, Max Soffar's life fell between the cracks. A sixth-grade dropout whose IQ tests pegged him as borderline mentally retarded, he grew up in Houston, where he was a petty burglar, an idiot-savant car thief, and a low-level, if highly imaginative, police snitch. He spent four years as a child, he says, "in the nuthouse in Austin," where he remembers the guards putting on human cockfights: They would lock two eleven-year-olds in the same cell, egg them on, and bet on which one of them would be able to walk out. Max ran away, and it's been pretty much downhill from there.

For the past twenty-three years, since confessing to a cold-blooded triple murder at a Houston bowling alley, Max has been at his final station on the way: the Polunsky Unit in Livingston, Texas. But he long ago recanted that confession, and many people, including an ever-growing number of Houston-area law enforcement officers, think he didn't commit the crime. They say he merely told the cops what they wanted to hear after three days of interrogation without a lawyer present. At the very least, they say, Max's case is an example of everything that's wrong with the system. In the words of my friend, Steve Rambam, who is Max's pro bono private investigator, "I'm not anti–death penalty; I'm just anti-the-wrong-guy-getting-executed." Another observer troubled by Max's case is Fifth Circuit Court of Appeals judge Harold R. DeMoss, Jr., who wrote in 2002, after hearing Max's last appeal, "I have lain awake nights agonizing over the enigmas, contradictions, and ambiguities" in the record.

Chief among these Kafkaesque elements is the fact that Max's state-appointed attorney was the late Joe Cannon, who was infamous for sometimes sleeping through his clients' capital murder trials. Cannon managed to stay awake for Max's, but he did not bother to interview the one surviving witness who might have cleared him. There are, incidentally, ten men on death row who were clients of Cannon's.

Then there's the evidence—or the total lack of it. Jim Schropp, a Washington, D.C., lawyer who's been handling Max's case for over ten years, also on a pro bono basis, says it seemed cut-and-dried when he initially reviewed the file. "But the more we looked into it," he told me, "the facts and the confession didn't match up." Schropp discovered that there was no physical evidence linking Max to the crime. No eyewitnesses who placed him at the scene or saw him do it. No fingerprints. No ballistics. Two police lineups in which Max was not identified by the witness. Polygraph tests he passed, which have now gone missing. If the facts had been before them, Schropp says, no jurors would have believed that the prosecution's case had eliminated all reasonable doubt. "When you peel away the layers of the onion," he says, "you find the rotten core."

Okay, so what about the confession? Rambam says that when Max was arrested on August 5, 1980, for speeding on a stolen motorcycle, it was the third or fourth time he'd been caught for various offenses, and he thought he could deal his way out again, as he'd done before. The bowling alley murders had been highly publicized, and Max had seen the police sketch of the perpetrator, which he thought resembled a friend and sometime running buddy. Max and the friend were on the outs—they'd agreed to rob their parents' houses, the friend reneged—so to get revenge and to help his own case in the process, Max volunteered that he knew something about the murders. Unfortunately, in his attempt to implicate his friend, he placed himself at the scene, and before long he became a target of the investigation himself. "The cops spoon-fed Max information, and he gave them what they wanted," Rambam says. "He was a confession machine. If he thought it would have helped him with the police, he would have confessed to kidnapping the Lindbergh baby." (That Lindbergh baby really gets around.)

The trouble is, Max's confession—actually, he made three different confessions—contained conflicting information. First, he claimed to be outside the bowling alley when the murders took place and that he only heard the shots. Then he said he was inside and saw it all go down. Then he said his friend shot two people and threw him the gun, whereupon he shot the other two; it was like a scene in an old western. The written record of Max's confession states that there were two gunmen, himself and his friend; the only surviving victim, the witness Joe Cannon didn't bother to interview, says there was only one. Max also told the cops that he and his friend had killed some people and buried them in a field. The cops used methane probes and search dogs and found nothing. He claimed that they had robbed several convenience stores, which turned out never to have been robbed. Best of all, when the cops told him that the bowling alley had been burglarized the night before the murders, Max confessed to that crime as well. What he didn't know was that the burglars had already been arrested. "We won't be needing that confession," the homicide detective reportedly told him. After signing the murder confession, Max asked the officers, "Can I go home now?"

You may be wondering: What about the friend? He was arrested solely on the basis of Max's confession but was released because there was no evidence (the same "evidence" was later considered good enough to put Max on death row). Nonetheless, at Max's trial, the prosecutor told the jury that the police knew that the friend was involved and that they planned to hunt him down once Max was dealt with. But it never happened, and for the past twenty-three years, the friend—who is the son of a Houston cop—has been living free as a bird, currently in Mississippi, with the long arm of the Texas law never once reaching out to touch him. Why? Good question. "It wasn't hard to run him down and pay him a visit," Rambam says. "I found his name in the phone book."

Why would someone confess to a crime he didn't commit? A cry for help? A drug-addled death wish? Perhaps it has to do with what the poet Kenneth Patchen once wrote: "There are so many little dyings, it doesn't matter which of them is death."

As my interview with Max was ending, he placed his hand against the glass. I did likewise. He said he would like me to be there with him at the execution if it happens. I hesitated. "You've come this far," he said. "Why go halfway?"

I promised him I would be there. It's a promise I would dearly love not to have to keep.

TWENTY-THREE

You gotta be kiddin', Sherlock," said a disappointed Ratso, when I called him. "All that work we did and now the cops have cracked the case?"

"Watson, Watson, Watson," I said. "There is a world of difference between 'cracking a case,' as you say, and someone merely making a confession. Remember, more than two hundred people confessed to kidnapping the Lindbergh baby, even though it was, of course, after our time. But if all those confessions were accurate and true, that's a big crowd of people at the Lindberghs' window."

"Who cares?" said Ratso. "Lindbergh was a Nazi."

"Ah, Watson, you do go right to the heart of things. The train of thought needs hardly to stop at your station, my dear friend."

"Thank you, Sherlock. Why all this shit about the Lindbergh baby anyway?"

"Because I *am* the Lindbergh baby. But right now I'm busy being Sherlock and I have good reason to believe that this current confession is a false one."

"You're kidding? How could you possibly know that? Do you know something about the man who confessed?"

"Not even his name, Watson. Not even the great McGovern, sometimes referred to as 'The Shadow,' knows the name of the confessor yet."

"Then how can you be so sure the confession is false?"

"Watson, you know my methods. I'm passionately anal retentive. And I particularly make a point of not divulging my methods to Jews or to the Irish. As Brendan Behan once remarked, 'The Jews and the Irish do not share a culture; they share a psychosis.' So I will not be sharing this information at this time with either you or McGovern. It is privileged and it must remain privileged until everything else is impossible."

"You're impossible."

"Watson, if I told you the reasoning behind why I strongly suspect the confession to be false, you would laugh and say it's so simple anybody could have figured that out. But anybody couldn't have figured it out, Watson! Only the great Sherlock could have tumbled to the truth so early in the investigation. And Sherlock's lonely secrets are secrets he must keep."

"Jump up my ass."

"Ah, my dear Watson, your earthy humor is ever a leavening agent, even at mankind's darkest hour!"

"Yeah, well, I'm not wasting all that legwork, Sherlock. If you won't tell me, I'll check with my own sauces. I have sauces, too, you know. Then I'll compare notes with McGovern. Then I'll come by your place later this afternoon and maybe you'll be a little more forthcoming with your dear friend Watson."

"Fine, Watson, fine."

As I believe I mentioned much earlier, Ratso had begun to be quite an irritant in my life. Because he had virtually no insight into the mind of the criminal, he would quite predictably go off on the wrong track at every opportunity. Like all of us, he was a creature of narrow habit. He was, unfortunately, also a creature of unpleasant habits. Maybe it's something in the nature of all relationships. What we once thought of as refreshing takes only a little time to become quite tedious. But it was far more than Ratso that was irritating me now. I firmly believed the cops had bought a false confession. If they considered the case closed, it would be most unfortunate. It would mean the real killer was still running loose on the street.

I met my friend Chinga Chavin at the Second Avenue Deli and chose not to burden him with details of the case. It was pleasant to be with someone besides Ratso for a change. I did not notice the small Band-Aids at Chinga's temples and around his thumbs. This was good. It meant he wasn't scratching and biting himself like a monkey on crack. Chinga's shrink had once referred to this behavior as "a grooming mechanism gone awry." It's almost like what happens, I thought, within the mind of a killer. Almost. What actually happens, only the killer could tell us, and in the matter at hand, I doubted seriously if the killer would ever confess.

It was about five-thirty by the time I got back to Vandam Street. Ratso was sitting on the stoop of the building, looking like a large, phlegm-colored, poisonous mushroom.

"Where the hell do you get a phlegm-colored jumpsuit in New York?" I asked.

"Hadassah Thrift Shop," he answered. "Do you want to know the name of the killer?"

"The killer or the poor bastard who confessed to a highly publicized crime he didn't commit?"

"The NYPD thinks they're one and the same, Sherlock."

"Then the NYPD is wrong," I said, as I unlocked the door of the building.

As in Heather Lay's building, the little freight elevator with one swinging exposed light bulb was not working. Unlike the one in Heather's building, this freight elevator hadn't worked in recent memory. Neither had I.

"A killer whose MO is to leave fiendishly dramatically staged death scenes," I continued, as we legged it up the darkened stairwell, "is not going to trot down to his local cop shop and turn himself in. Far from it, Watson. Right now the killer, far from feeling remorseful, is very probably luxuriating in the news of this false confession—"

"Sherlock, you don't know it's false! I haven't even told you the guy's name. It's Barry Russell, by the way. No previous rap sheet."

"An institutionalized mind wishing desperately to get back in prison, Watson, is only one reason for making a false confession. Climbing too many stairs could be one. No, no, no, Watson. The killer is still here, right here in the Village, and we must struggle forward with the investigation because we're getting closer to this evil-doer with every step that we take. Do you hear me, Watson?"

"No. I've got a Persian slipper in my ear."

"You'll have a Persian slipper in your ass if you don't move along a little faster."

The truth was, we really were getting closer to the killer. The mind behind five murders had already pretty much unmasked itself by this time. It was the kind of mind, I believed very strongly, that would never be satiated until the killer was caught.

We were not in the loft long enough for the espresso machine to finish humming "My Old Kentucky Home" when we had an unexpected knock upon the door. I looked at Ratso, he shrugged, and I looked at Sherlock, who didn't blink. Then I took a patient puff on my cigar and was about to walk over to the door when our visitors announced themselves.

"Police. Open up," said a voice.

"Tex," said another, more familiar voice. "It's Mort Cooperman."

When the cops arrive five minutes after you do, it's never a very good sign. It means they've got their beady little eyes trained closely on your comings and goings, and maybe even on your staying homes. I knew the visit was coming, of course. I just didn't know if

Cooperman wanted a cup of sugar or if he was trying to sell me something. I went over and opened the door.

"Sorry to keep you waiting," I said, as Cooperman and a plain-clothes dick I didn't know brushed past me into the room.

"No problem," said Cooperman, playing it straight. "We were in the neighborhood. Just thought I'd come by and borrow a cigar, if I might."

"I didn't know you smoked cigars," I said.

"I don't," said Cooperman.

His demeanor did not seem as gruff as usual. He was still his surly self, but he appeared to be a bit subdued. He introduced the other guy to me and Ratso, some kind of tech specialist named David Anderson. The other guy wandered about the loft as Cooperman wandered over to my desk. I maintained my position loitering between the desk and the door. It was cop etiquette. They could wander wherever the hell they wanted and I could loiter wherever the hell I wanted just as long as I didn't have to go with them when they left. Cooperman seemed on the verge of saying something when Ratso pulled his head out of the refrigerator long enough to pipe up himself.

"Hey, congratulations, officer," he said. "I hear the perp of those five murders has confessed."

"Forget it," said Cooperman, shooting Ratso a look so hard it caused him to close the door to the refrigerator.

"Yeah," Ratso continued obliviously, "but this Barry Russell guy. I thought you had him in custody."

"We did," said Cooperman. "But there's been another murder."

TWENTY-FOUR

There'd been another murder, all right, and Cooperman's grim mood spoke worlds that it must've been a doozy. Cooperman had been on the circuit for a while and seen just about everything. If I hadn't known better I would've said that he seemed almost a bit shaken up over recent events. For a pro like him, it was highly unusual. He grilled us for a while—where we were last night; where we were this morning; what we did; who we did it with. Maybe it was me, but it didn't really seem as if his heart was in it. But all that was about to change. And fast.

"Victim's name was Ron Lucas," Cooperman intoned. "Lived near here on Bank Street. Died sometime around midnight or the early hours of the morning."

"How do you know it's connected to the other murders?" asked Ratso.

"We'll get to that, pal," said Cooperman, raising his hand like a traffic cop to encourage Ratso to pull his lips together.

Up to this point, I had taken some comfort from Ratso's presence in the loft. It hadn't really changed the cops' methodology. Anderson was milling about, after spending some time adjusting the position

131

of the puppethead on the fireplace mantel. Cooperman, as always, when he really had something, was taking his sweet time. But Ratso did provide a buffer to what certainly would have been more intense scrutiny upon the Kinkster had he not been there. Unfortunately, he did not really know how or when to talk to a cop. He conversed with them just like they were normal people, which, of course, is always a rather tragic mistake.

"How many cigars you got at the moment?" Cooperman suddenly asked.

"Enough," I said. "I don't know exactly. They're in Sherlock's head."

"They're where?"

"On the desk. In Sherlock's head."

"All Cubans?"

"Yes," I said. "But I'm not supporting their economy; I'm burning their fields."

"You got those kind where one end's shaped like a torpedo?"

"Yeah."

"What're they called?"

"Lots of Cuban cigars are shaped like a torpedo. What I have in stock are Montecristo Number 2's. What is this? A customs bust?"

"Mind if I have a look at one? The Montecristo Number 2?"

"No problem," I said, and I walked over to the desk, lifted Sherlock's cap, and peered down into the empty space where anybody who chooses to be a private investigator keeps his brains. I didn't like the way Cooperman was dragging this out. It was mildly troubling to me because I suspected it was building to something that I wasn't going to want to put in my pipe and smoke. There were fewer cigars in there than I'd thought, but that always seemed to be the case. When you smoke incessantly, you tend to lose count. I found a Monte 2 and took it over to where Cooperman was standing and forked it over to him.

"No cigar band?" he asked. "Why?"

"Because they take them off before they ship them so they can get them through customs. It's illegal, Sergeant. Do I need a lawyer present?"

"Not yet," he said.

Cooperman called Anderson over, and holding the cigar very delicately, placed it in a plastic evidence bag. To paraphrase Bob Dylan, something was happening, but I didn't know what it was. I glanced over at Ratso. He shrugged again. Anderson went back to strolling around the loft, touching the dust on surfaces, sitting in chairs, straightening furniture, almost like a prospective buyer or a building inspector. It seemed as if it were his loft and Ratso and I were being interviewed as potential subletters. But you can't stop a cop from being a cop. It gives the appearance that you have something to hide.

You could almost smell the coal burning inside Cooperman's head, feeding the engines of doubt and truth and progress in the investigation. Like Sherlock, like myself, he wasn't yet ruling anyone or anything out. That was to his credit, I thought. Now you could almost see the steam coming out of his ears. He had to be debating how much he should say.

"Espresso anyone?" said Ratso, with an exaggerated lilt and lisp to his voice. He got no takers. Cooperman's more relaxed body language, however, seemed to indicate that he'd come to some kind of conclusion. I doubted, though, that he would really take us into his confidence. More likely, he would just give us enough rope to either hang ourselves or start up a rope factory.

"The murders seem to be getting more and more frenzied," Cooperman said. "This last one was a zoo and a half. Rice strewn all over the place—"

"Ricin?" asked Ratso.

"Rice, you idiot!" said Cooperman, in a momentary lapse of control.

"'She picks up some rice from the place where a wedding has been,'" I recited.

"Quite," said Anderson, who'd been listening from across the room.

"We needed the cigar for comparison purposes. The lab will soon tell us if the cigars used in the murders were Cuban."

"How do you murder somebody with cigars?" I asked, not unreasonably.

Cooperman looked over to Anderson. Now it was Anderson's turn to shrug. Cooperman walked over to the window and looked down grimly into the darkening street. When he spoke at last, it was in a soft, almost world-weary voice.

"This sounds comical unless you've seen it with your own eyes. A guy with his hands duct-taped behind his back. Three cigars shoved down his throat. One in his mouth that had been lit but gone out. One screwed into each of his nostrils. One shoved up his ass. One screwed into each ear. Nine in all. Nine torpedo-shaped cigars without bands, which look just like the one you gave us and just like the one you're smoking now, so we suspect they're Cuban. Cigar jammed into every fucking orifice. Cause of death, asphyxiation by cigar, or multiple cigars, shoved down his throat."

"You gotta be kiddin'," said Ratso. "No one murders somebody like that."

"Somebody did last night on Bank Street," said Cooperman.

"So what's the rice got to do with it?" Ratso persisted.

"We don't know," said Cooperman. "We found a box of Uncle Ben's Instant Rice beside the body at the scene. The box had been scribbled on in a strange way and we're not sure what, if anything, it means. Where it says 'Uncle Ben's,' the 'U' has been enclosed at the top to make it an 'O,' and the 'n,' 'c,' and 'e' have been marked out. Also, the apostrophe and the 's' at the end of Ben's have been marked out. So it reads, 'Ol Ben,' whatever that's supposed to mean. Could be important, could be nothing."

I had thought Ratso would pick up on it, and he did. I had hoped he would have the good sense to keep it to himself, but, of course, he didn't. I was about to say, "I'll take that espresso now," to try to head him off at the pass, but he probably wouldn't have paid any attention anyway. His Watsonlike face was already aglow with the excitement of having put two and two together and coming up with Catch-22. He was so clueless there was just no stopping him when he thought he'd discovered a clue.

"Hey, wait a minute!" Ratso shouted. "This guy's name was Lucas?"

"That's right," said Anderson, who'd wandered back over. "Ron Lucas."

"That's it!" Ratso shouted again. "That's why the Uncle Ben's rice was used! The letters were changed to Ol Ben and the guy's last name was Lucas!"

"And?" said Cooperman, beginning to become irritated with Ratso.

"Don't you see?" Ratso crowed. "It's 'Ol' Ben Lucas'! It's one of the Kinkstah's most famous songs! It's the first song he ever wrote!"

"It's a stupid song," I said, trying to deflect where this was going. "I wrote it when I was eleven years old."

"It means the killer knew Kinky's song!" Ratso nattered on, totally oblivious to how deeply enmeshed I was becoming in the dragnet that was Cooperman's mind.

"'Ol' Ben Lucas,'" said Cooperman slowly, trying it on for size.

"Maybe the song had something to do with the killer screwing the cigars into Lucas's nostrils?" Ratso suggested.

"Maybe it had something to do with the killer shoving the cigar up his ass," I said.

But nobody was listening. Ratso was breaking his arm patting himself on the back for discovering such an important and vital clue. The two homicide dicks, to my horror, appeared to be taking Ratso a good bit more seriously now.

"'Ol' Ben Lucas,'" Cooperman said again, directing his full attention to Ratso. "Think you could hum a few bars?"

"Actually, we'll need the lyrics, too," put in Anderson, moving closer to Ratso.

"Well, I don't know," said Ratso, with mock humility. "I can't really sing that well."

"It's a stupid song," I said. Nobody heard me.

"You do *know* the song?" Cooperman asked Ratso.

"Of course!" said Ratso. "Everybody does."

"At least you and the killer know it," said Cooperman. "And, of course, Tex here, who, you say, *wrote* it?"

"When he was eleven years old," said Ratso, beaming with all the admiration of a proud parent.

"Come on," said Cooperman to Ratso. "Sing a little bit of it."

"Okay," said Ratso, like a nervous contestant in some game show. "Here goes."

With that he sang the chorus of the song for the cops. He gave a flawless performance, I had to admit. Any five-year-old, of course, could have done the same. What Ratso sang is as follows:

"Ol' Ben Lucas, Had a lotta mucus
Comin' right outta his nose.
He'd pick and pick 'til it made you sick
But back again it grows."

"That's it?" said Cooperman after a long pause. He looked like somebody had hit him with a hammer.

"Yeah," said Ratso. "That was the chorus."

"It's a catchy little booger," said Cooperman, egging Ratso on. "And who said you couldn't sing? You were great. Wasn't he great, Sergeant?"

"Best thing I've heard since Joey Ramone died," said Anderson.

"That was the chorus," said Cooperman. "How many verses are there?"

"One," said Ratso, a bit defensively, I thought.

"One chorus, one verse," said Cooperman, almost gleefully. "We've heard the chorus, let's hear the verse. C'mon. Don't be shy. Let 'er rip."

For a moment I thought Ratso was beginning to dimly suspect that this whole thing might not have been such a great idea. Perhaps he could see me in the background giving him the dagger-across-the-throat sign. Perhaps he'd come to realize on his own that this audience was not a group of relatives at a bar mitzvah party. This was the literal-minded, anal-retentive, humorless, colorless, culture-bound, park-between-the-lines law. I saw by the look in his eyes that he wasn't exactly sure whether or not these were his people. But now, of course, it was too late. He soldiered on.

"'When it's cotton-pickin' time in Texas,'" he sang, "'it's booger-pickin' time for Ben.'"

Cooperman was clapping his hands in encouragement and nodding over to Anderson to join in. And my mind was whirring with only one thought: The killer knew the fucking song.

"He'd raise that finger, mean and hostile
Stick it in that waiting nostril.
Here he comes with a green one once again."

Cooperman applauded the little performance heartily. Sergeant Anderson joined in. Ratso was back to being Ratso. Once again, he trusted his crowd. He was luxuriating in this spectacle, like Wayne

Newton on a Vegas Saturday night, even throwing a little salute to his audience. He did everything but blow kisses. Then Cooperman stopped applauding and turned to me.

"Goddamnit, Tex," he said ruefully. "I almost thought you were out of it."

TWENTY-FIVE

The good news, I suppose, was that Cooperman didn't take me out of there in bracelets that night. He merely warned me once again not to leave the city. Most New Yorkers, of course, would've found a warning like that to be quite unnecessary, even redundant. Most of them believe that if they ever left the city, they'd fall right off the face of the earth. That's how far we've come. I'd come pretty far myself, I thought, as pertains to the matter at hand. I had my own ideas about where the investigation into the six murders was leading, and, of course, the cops had theirs. They believed that I, or one of my minions, was the perpetrator. Oddly enough, I did not necessarily disagree with them.

The "Ol' Ben Lucas Clue," as Ratso now referred to it, was ridiculous on the face of it. There were people all over the world who'd been practically raised with the song by their hip, baby-boomer parents. The parents, no doubt, were pretty much beyond the age profile of serial killers. But infants back in the seventies and eighties whose folks had been fans of the Kinkster's fell perfectly into the age range. And the song, deceptively simple in music and lyrics, like a slightly twisted childhood nursery rhyme, stayed with you for life. Unfortu-

139

nately, it had gotten very little radio play over the years, having been passed along in the oral tradition from parents to their children. Therefore, it had not been a financial pleasure for the Kinkster.

While the song seemed absurd, both as a song and as a clue to a horrific string of murders, it might, I reflected, be the perfect sound-track for a psychopathic mind. Then, if you added the "death by cigar" angle to the "Ol' Ben Lucas Clue," well, I was forced to admit you were starting to get precariously close to the Kinkster's ZIP code. Was somebody trying to implicate me? Was somebody merely taunt-ing my vaunted powers of observation as a much-celebrated amateur private investigator? Or was it possible that there existed in this uni-verse a serial killer discerning in terms of music and cigars who, though obviously quite bitter, had somehow managed to retain his sense of humor?

There was another little matter I was wrangling with in the days immediately following the visit from Cooperman. It was my growing belief that I was now being kept under surveillance by the NYPD. You could call it paranoia and you might be right, but there were too many little giveaways for me to discount the idea. I'm not contending that they had had a tail on me since childhood, though knowing Cooperman and Fox it was certainly possible; I'm simply wondering why they didn't approach Ratso when he was waiting for me in front of the building? The logical answer is that by that time they were already tailing me, thus accounting for Cooperman's quick knock on the door only minutes after my return to the loft.

And where the hell was Fox? I'd asked Cooperman and he'd been very vague. And Anderson was some kind of tech, apparently. Not that his behavior had been particularly uncoplike, but he had wan-dered all over the loft, precisely in the manner of someone whose job it was to surreptitiously hide a bug—and I'm not talking about a cockroach. The more I thought about it, the more convinced I became that the loft, indeed, had been bugged. It wouldn't be the first time, of course. Rambam had even surreptitiously bugged the place once himself, in the affair McGovern had faithfully chronicled and dubbed "Spanking Watson." An electronic bug could present problems, all right, but at least I could check to determine its presence, and if in fact it was there, I could either remove it or possibly use it to my own advantage.

Being tailed was another matter, however. Rambam, I knew, was a master at detecting a tail, eluding a tail, and, of course, getting lots of tail. Unfortunately, Rambam was currently somewhere in Cambodia, busy with a challenging case of grand theft water buffalo. I couldn't just call him on the shoe phone, so I had to rely on my own rudimentary surveillance skills. Or maybe not. In a flash, I called Kent Perkins, my left coast PI, who'd played a seminal role in a recent adventure McGovern had tediously scrutinized and titled "The Prisoner of Vandam Street." I couldn't very well call Kent from the loft to discuss being bugged if, indeed, I'd been bugged. So I put on my colorful Indian longcoat and got my cowboy hat and grabbed a few cigars out of Sherlock's head. I would be easy to spot, but what the hell. I was only going to take a brisk walk to a pay phone somewhere, and if they could spot me, maybe I could spot them. Too bad they didn't make rearview mirrors for cowboy hats.

I started to leave the cat in charge but quickly realized once again that that would not be possible. It's funny how we seem to internalize all the things that really matter. Creatures of narrow habit. Creatures of sad habit.

I ankled it down the stairs and out into the street. It was the middle of the afternoon and what appeared to be a plain-wrapped squad car was parked about a hundred yards to my left. A guy inside looked up casually and then turned his attention, perhaps a little too quickly, back to reading a newspaper. I hooked a right and goose-stepped for the corner.

TWENTY-SIX

That Ol' Ben Lucas business is either some kind of incredible coincidence," said Kent Perkins, "or somebody's seriously trying to frame you."

"You're the PI," I said. "What do you think?"

"I don't believe in coincidences," said Kent. "Where are you now?"

"I'm at a pay phone on the corner a block and a half from the loft, pretending not to see a guy in a plain-wrapped squad car who's pretending not to see me. I guess I didn't really think they'd actually put me under surveillance, so I didn't dress for the occasion. I'm wearing a black cowboy hat and a long, red Indian coat made from a blanket on the res. In this outfit, the blind sheik Abdul bin Bubba could probably tail me."

"Could work to your advantage. You could work a variation on the old cowboy-hat-behind-the-boulder trick. It always worked for Tom Mix."

Kent proceeded to lay out an urban, modern version of an old ploy straight out of a western movie. It sounded fairly preposterous but it might be crazy enough to work, I told Kent, as I watched the tail pretend to look at the address of a nearby building. What a wonderful world, I thought. Here I am in New York, being framed apparently by the sickest psycho in the city, and my pal Kent Perkins, probably driving Dean Martin's old sand-over-sable Rolls through Beverly Hills, is giving me advice on how to elude the cops.

"You can't go back to the loft," he said. "There's a chance the place *is* bugged and if you try to disassemble the bug you tip your hand and look guilty. You've got to stay with a friend for a few days and keep out of sight. The cops are probably just messing with your head. I can't believe they'd really think you could be the murderer."

"That's why you're not a cop," I said.

I cradled the blower and casually legged it up the street in the direction away from the tail. Maybe it wasn't that big a deal after all. If Abbie Hoffman managed to elude the Feds for years as an underground fugitive, shaking this tail should be a piece of cake. But what if I did elude them this time? They'd only find me again. And why would they waste the time and manpower to tail somebody twenty-four hours a day if they didn't strongly suspect him? Meanwhile, of course, the real killer was running loose somewhere, maybe looking out at you from some window at Starbucks, or perhaps sitting alone at a table at the Carnegie Deli, possibly pretending to eat a bagel. I began to see even more clearly why people made false confessions. If enough people suspect you long enough and hard enough, you begin to almost believe that the real killer is you.

It was starting to rain by the time I got to the little neighborhood bar called "The Ear," so named because the letter "B" of the word "Bar" was half burned out, as, of course, were most of the clientele. The place was not crowded, but it was full enough to hide a cowboy who was holding his hat out deliberately from behind a boulder in order to draw fire or at least a little attention. The guy who was tailing me parked directly across the street from The Ear, now making no pretense about reading the paper. The relationship between the tail and the tailee was a little bit like love, I reflected, as I entered the place: After the period of courtship is over, you just get right down to it.

There are icons in this world such as Elvis, Jesus, Che Guevara, and James Dean. Then there are cult celebrities who do not stir instant crowd hysteria but may cause a number of individuals to whisper, "Isn't that Toulouse-Lautrec?" It is that latter galaxy of smaller stars to which I belong, but even that can have its advantages. Fortunately, Mal, the guy who ran the place, was there behind the bar. I had a few brief words with him, ordered a Guinness, and found an empty table right by the window, taking a seat with my back against the street. This, I figured, had to be a surveillance cop's dream. Here was a guy in a bright red Indian blanket, a big black cowboy hat, and smoking a big cigar, sitting at a table right by the window. You could tail a guy like that in your sleep. That was exactly what I wanted the cop to think.

After I'd been nursing the Guinness for a few minutes, Mal made a small announcement to the bar patrons. Shortly after that, I got up and left my drink and headed in the obvious direction of the dumper. Three or four customers gravitated to the same area, whereupon we congregated in a small hallway out of sight of the prying eyes of the street. What Mal and I had cooked up was a typical small pub amusement: a Kinky Friedman look-alike contest. I selected a Jewish-looking ectomorph with a mustache, who was probably an accountant or a homosexual, or, very possibly, a serial killer himself, and I gave him my hat and my coat and stuck a cigar in his mouth. He walked back to my table by the window and sat down in my chair to a light smattering of applause, thereby winning a free round of drinks for himself and his friends, if he had any, which I rather doubted. I took the opportunity to put on a dark, nondescript raincoat and don a black beret that may well have been forlornly hanging there for many years, depending on whether it had been left by

Lennon or Lenin. Then I scooted like a dog out the back door into a welcome wall of rain.

Evading an NYPD surveillance team—I say team, because though I only saw the one guy, I didn't know who or what else was out there—is always an exhilarating experience. It's a better high than closing on a house or getting a divorce. Jewish divorces, incidentally, are always the most expensive. That's because they're worth it. At any rate, I wandered through the rain-wept streets of the Village for a while, just to be sure that I'd really shaken the tail. I hadn't given a lot of thought to what my next amusement would be. I figured I'd just drift over in the general direction of McGovern's place on Jane Street. It was a step up from Ratso's with the only downside being that you usually had to repeat everything two times, which of course is redundant because if you repeat something that is two times. The serial killer, it should be noted, had now struck six times.

Walking around in the rain connects all the dots in the world and sometimes helps you see things from a different slant, almost as if those little raindrops really know where they're going. As if any of us really know where we're going. So I wondered as I wandered, as the rain continued to fall, as the wheels and the world continued to spin, as paper boats continued to sail upon the asphalt sea, as water turned to wine, and wine turned to blood, and the day turned to night, and lovers turned to each other, and men and women turned gay, and I turned right on Christopher Street.

The "Ol' Ben Lucas Clue," as Ratso had called it, was what was bothering me. Assuming that rather obliquely obvious message had not been left by someone with only a passing familiarity with that song, but rather a passing familiarity with me, it indicated that the killer had to emanate from a relatively small universe of human beings, if, indeed, you want to call a killer like this human. Indeed, if you walked in the rain a while and thought about it, the killer was just about as human as it gets. To paraphrase my father, the term we criminologists like to use for this kind of killer is "a sick fuck."

The combination of the song and the Cuban cigars was highly problematical for the Kinkster. It did not necessarily portend that the murderer was a Village Irregular or somebody close to me. A deranged fan, for instance, could have been capable of the same behavior. There were lots of deranged fans out there, as Bob Dylan, Dwight Yoakam, John Cale, or virtually any thinking man's rock star will tell you. We all tend to have a little deranged fan in us, to overidentify with our field of study, thereby incurring the rain-barrel effect, in which one more tiny imagined slight can produce horrific results. In other words, the killer didn't necessarily have to know me. The problem was that I was pretty sure that he did.

We all wear masks. But a monster of this magnitude wears a mask that is all but impenetrable to the naked eye. Was Chinga capable of these acts? Were Mick Brennan or Pete Myers? Even Rambam, Ratso, McGovern? How does anybody ever know until the fateful moment the killer lifts his hand, when the mask falls to the bloody floor? If a human being is capable of these actions, as was clearly the case, then any one of us would appear to be abundantly capable of crawling into the demon's skull for a while, getting behind the wheel, and going for a little ride. It's not so strange really. Especially when it's raining.

I don't know how long I roamed the streets like a rambling hunchback, but I eventually found myself in the familiar environs of the Corner Bistro and Jane Street. I had no idea how Cooperman would react to the news that I had eluded their surveillance. Would he merely stake out the loft? Would he redouble efforts to find me? Would he put out an APB to all ships at sea, close the airports, ban smoking in neighborhood bars? I was soaking wet by this time, cold, and exhausted. The thrill of outwitting the cops had just about worn off. As Kris Kristofferson once observed, "Freedom's just another word for nothin' left to lose." As somebody else once said, "The policeman is your friend." As Bukowski once said, "Run with the hunted." As Meatloaf said, "Two out of three ain't bad."

I was hanging by spit by the time I got to McGovern's building. Not only did I feel like a fugitive on the run, but it was highly unnerving as the realization had sunken in that the sickest fuck in the city knew a great deal more about me than I knew about him. 2B or not 2B, I thought as I drilled McGovern's buzzer about eleven times, that really was the fucking question. And the answer, apparently, was that it was not 2B, for McGovern wasn't home. Visions of Ratso's skidmarked couch flitted briefly through my mind, but were rejected almost as quickly as they came, no pun intended. I had to think rationally, I told myself. After all, I hadn't broken any law by evading the cops because ostensibly I wasn't supposed to be aware that they were following me. What a joke, I thought. The cops following me had pretended like they weren't following me while I was pretending like I didn't know I was being followed. It seemed very much like an atheist who goes through life vociferously denying the existence of God right up until the moment the celestial shit hits the fan.

I resorted at last to the old Kinkster method of pushing every buzzer on the wall. It worked like a Samoan charm. The door buzzed like a large bee, I walked in from the rain, ankled it up one flight of stairs, walked to the far end of the hallway, and sat down on the comfortable, carpeted floor, my back resting against McGovern's warm door. I must have either nodded out or passed out, but when I awoke I was mildly surprised to see the jolly green giant standing over me.

"Get inside," said McGovern. "The cops're looking for you everywhere."

I dutifully followed the big man into the relatively small apartment and immediately plopped down on the sofa Frederick Exley had slept on, that large, soft, salmon-colored sofa that had been shipped across the Atlantic twice in its lifetime. When I looked up, McGovern had pulled up a chair close to the sofa and poured us each an adult portion of what I was sure was strong snakepiss. He handed me a glass, I downed about half, and it shook me by the shoulders.

"Are you positive you weren't followed here by the cops?" he asked with a surprising degree of intensity.

"Positive," I said. "Been wandering free as a bird for hours. I shook 'em at The Ear late this afternoon. The device was a Kinky Friedman impersonator contest."

"That's too fucking bad," said McGovern almost bitterly.

"Why is that?" I said.

"Because the seventh murder went down about three hours ago."

TWENTY-SEVEN

The part of me that's Indian is very wise," McGovern was saying as he made coffee the following morning.

"And what is the part of you that's Indian telling you?" I inquired.

"It says, 'Pale face kemosabe in a heap big pile of deep Nixon.'"

"I see. And what does the Irish part of you say?"

"The Irish part of me says, 'Put a little Bushmill's in the coffee.'"

"Very sensible. And I take it the Indian part is in basic agreement with the Irish part as pertains to putting some firewater in the coffee?"

"That's about the only thing they both *do* agree on. By the way, what is your proud Hebraic background telling you?"

"Take out life insurance now," I said.

The situation, however, was really no joking matter. I longed for the days when I was a lonely, loveless amateur private investigator living with an antisocial cat in a draughty loft beneath the pounding hooves of a lesbian dance class. All that was gone now, I reflected. Flying far away somewhere with Holden Caulfield's ducks and Martin Luther King's dreams.

"It's most unfortunate," McGovern was pontificating, "that you eluded the police surveillance at the time that you did. Had they still been tailing you at the time of the seventh murder, it would've cleared you beyond a doubt. But with them already suspicious of you, and then you evade the surveillance within hours of the crime, it looks really bad from their point of view. Surely you see that."

"Nixon happens," I said, more cavalierly than I felt. Cavalier was about the only way to go at a time like this, I thought. I recalled that Cavalier had been the name of Breaker Morant's horse. Breaker was a war hero with poetry in his saddlebags and the Brits had killed him for it. Happened every day. Good, even great, innocent people killed under the charade of what they called the law by gutless bastards. What chance did a maverick like myself have in a world like this? I couldn't hide at McGovern's forever. I'd either have to turn myself in to the cops or turn the key of my loft over to Winnie again and cash in my airline miles, which, of course, I didn't have. I only had miles. Miles and miles of bathroom tiles with green and hungry crocodiles waiting at the corners of my eyes.

"What do you know about the seventh murder?" I asked McGovern.

"Much bloodier, less musical," he said. "Stabbed about a zillion times, mostly in the groin area. They're not telling me everything, of course. There was, incidentally, a note left next to the body this time. Homicide is keeping its contents very close to the vest, however."

"Did it say, 'Support mental health or I'll eat you'?"

"Cheer up," said McGovern. "Cannibalism can't be far behind."

"But why are the cops after me? Why aren't they busy pursuing the killer?"

"That should be obvious, isn't it?"

"Not to me. They couldn't be stupid enough to believe I'm the killer. Cooperman's smarter than that. In fact, he's far too savvy to think I killed these people."

"I feel sure he doesn't really believe you killed anybody."

"I'm not so sure he won't bust me anyway. Highly publicized, serial killings create a certain climate of urgency around any cop shop. Sometimes common sense is overtaken by the desire to find a perpetrator. Sometimes any perpetrator will do. It happens often enough."

"But that's not what's happening here," said McGovern, as he brought me a steaming cup of coffee laced with a double shot of Black Bush. "What's happening here is that they think you know something you're not telling them."

"I do."

TWENTY-EIGHT

After McGovern had left for work, I lay on the couch for a while staring at the photo of Carole Lombard that hung on the brick wall next to the fireplace. Something about her eyes reminded me of someone. Was it Heather, or was it someone I loved long ago and was lucky enough to still love today? Or was it someone else? I wasn't sure, but whoever it was, she was trying to tell me something. This made no sense at all, of course, but that's how I read it. A woman I knew, or had once known, was trying to communicate with my soul through the eyes of a dead movie star. What's wrong with that? It wasn't half as crazy as this murder investigation. The dead bodies were stacking up all over the Village, it seemed, and the two entities that might have half a chance of catching the killer, the NYPD and the Kinkster, were sharing information almost as well as the FBI and the CIA. And the murders were happening so fast it was almost like the killer was expecting to be caught. The only thing I felt certain of was that the killer would not stop until apprehended. An artist knows when to stop; a killer never does.

It's the little things, they say, that are important in life. The little things, of course, are also important in death. Based solely on the sketchy nature of McGovern's initial sources, it was very difficult to draw a great deal of enlightenment. In other words, I needed what the cops had. Conversely, they needed what I had, though, no doubt, they didn't quite see it that way. It was a shame we both weren't better team players.

As I saw it, my options were quite few. If the cops were actively looking for me, the loft on Vandam Street would most certainly be staked out. So I could hole up at McGovern's for a while, then move from safe house to safe house like a good Robin Hood or a bad Saddam. It was unlikely, however, that the case was ever going to be solved if my lifestyle devolved to that of a fugitive from justice. Sooner or later, it appeared, I would have to confront the authorities and face the music. Parking my ego at the door, it was nevertheless my firm opinion that, unless they got very lucky, the NYPD was not likely to bring this killer to justice.

In the past there were many times when I hadn't seen eye to eye with Detective Sergeants Cooperman and Fox and their minions, but this was the first time I'd been so totally shut out of the crime scenes, so utterly excommunicated from the official investigation. Kent Perkins had said that it appeared as if I were being framed, but I didn't quite see it that way. It felt more to me like I was being taunted. Arrogance, indubitably, is the hallmark of every murderer. This one seemed to be challenging me to take my best shot.

From the vantage point of McGovern's couch I reviewed what I knew of the victims, the clues, the virtual leap of deduction I would have to make, not being privy to all the pieces of the puzzle. Beginning with the very first victim's wallet being discovered in my loft, the case had started by drawing me into it, and now had transformed itself into some fashion of horrific tarbaby that seemed determined not to let me go. Where did one find a knitting needle in the haystack of the city? Where did one find the savagery to drive it into a victim's brain? The anger to lop a man's shillelagh off and let him bleed to death? To waste nine good Cuban cigars in the wasting of a human being was an act of unspeakable evil. I thought again of Ratso obliviously singing the catchy, if somewhat crude, little children's song to the cops. As author of "Ol' Ben Lucas," I rather resented its use to mock the dead. But it was unmistakable. Converting the Uncle Ben's Rice box to read Ol Ben. The victim's name had been Lucas. The killer knew the song. The killer knew I smoked Cuban cigars. Did that, of itself, mean that the killer necessarily knew me? Could he be a vigilante, I thought, of the very worst, most primitive kind? A killer who, indeed, may walk about in society while inside, his mind and his soul are unraveling into the depths of depravity? Carole Lombard caught my eye again. What was she trying to tell me?

I must have nodded out for a while, because when McGovern suddenly burst into the place much earlier than I'd expected, I almost did a double-back-flip off the couch. He seemed to be in a state of almost unbridled excitement as he helped me up from the floor. I took a seat finally in an overstuffed rocking chair beside a pile of old newspapers that seemed to reach the sky.

"What the hell is it, McGovern?" I said at last.

"The note!" he ejaculated. "The note!"

"What note?"

"The one that was found beside the body of the seventh murder victim."

"Ah, yes, Watson. The much-heralded hate mail from the hand of a killer."

"A source at the NYPD just provided me with the information with the express understanding that it is to be off the record and not to be printed."

"Very wise, Watson, very wise."

"I didn't want to reveal the note's contents over the phone, so I rushed right over."

"Very wise, Watson, very wise."

"Okay. You're sitting down. You're ready for this?" McGovern flipped through his little reporter's notebook.

"I've been ready for about fifty-nine years, Watson. What the hell did the note say?"

"Hang on a minute. Let me find it." He flipped frantically through the notebook.

"Watson, your organizational skills are to be highly commended. You are a veritable machine, my dear friend."

"I copied the note verbatim from my source. Just a minute. I had it right here."

"I'll probably have passed away before you find it."

"Here it is!" said McGovern triumphantly, the big man holding the tiny notebook in the air. "Ready for this?"

"No," I said. "Give me a little time to prepare myself."

McGovern walked purposefully to the center of the room. Holding the notebook in front of him with both hands so as not to miss a word, he read as follows:

"'When it gets too kinky for the rest of the world, it's getting just right for me.'"

TWENTY-NINE

fter McGovern had triumphantly trotted back to work, I was left to ponder the imponderables. I figured that the little homicide note chased away any lingering doubts the NYPD might've had about the Kinkster's involvement in the case. They had their person of interest and that was me. I couldn't really blame Cooperman. If I'd been him I would've thought the same. From the dead man's wallet in the loft, to the "Ol' Ben Lucas" scenario, to my eluding police surveillance at precisely the wrong window of time, to the general kinky quality of the crimes themselves, to "When it gets too kinky for the rest of the world, it's getting just right for me," there was a pattern here that even Ratso couldn't have missed. Whether I'd done the crimes myself (which, of course, I hadn't), or whether I was merely being set up, I could see why I'd become the principal person of interest in the eyes of the cops. I had to admit that even I was getting a little interested in myself.

Not long after the door had slammed on McGovern's large, luminous, white buttocks, I broke into his bottle of Black Bush and began pacing back and forth across the little apartment. I had to be sure, I thought. And to be sure, I had to get into the mind of the killer. A

159

murderer who was taunting someone was different from a murderer who was trying to frame someone, even though it was too nuanced a point to register heavily with the cops. The difference, however, was crucial because it went to motivation. When it comes to crime-solving, I'll take motivation every time. Carole Lombard smiled that smart, savvy smile at me and I knew I was on the right track.

I drank some more of McGovern's snakepiss and I thought again about the note left at the scene of the crime. It meant a lot more to me than it did, no doubt, to the cops. It was a line from a fairly obscure song on a fairly obscure album I'd recorded almost thirty years ago. The song was called "Kinky" and it was written by the great Ronnie Hawkins. We'd recorded the song at Shangri-La, The Band's private studio near Malibu. The musicians included Rick Danko, Levon Helm, Richard Manuel, Garth Hudson, Lowell George, Ron Wood, Van Dyke Parks, Dr. John, Ringo Starr, and Eric Clapton. Some are dead and some are living. In my life I've loved them all.

Yet while "Ol' Ben Lucas" was known to half the civilized world, with the possible exception of Sergeant Cooperman, who was, apparently, ignorant of my talents, the same could not be said for "Kinky." "Kinky," for all its merits, was a song known only by that small, twisted group of people I like to refer to as "insects trapped in amber." This constituted a very tiny universe, indeed. If the killer knew the song, he very likely knew more about me than I knew about myself. Either the murderer had known me for a long time, or else he'd really done his homework. Today, of course, with the Internet, any serial killer worth the name can easily bone up on his field of study. That widened the universe a little, but only a little. The thing that was truly haunting me, however, was not the scenario of the killer knowing a lot about me. It was the feeling, based purely on the abstract nature of the crimes, that I knew the killer.

By the time McGovern returned that evening, the bottle of Black Bush was almost empty and Carole Lombard had started winking at me, which I took as a sign. Over the years and miles, from the world of the dead to the world of the dimly lit, she knew something, all right. And this time, though I may have been walking on my knuckles, I had more than an inkling that I knew what it was.

"Here's my question," I said to McGovern, as he lumbered in the door. "Just how well do we truly know the people who are closest to us?"

"Here's my question," said McGovern, as he walked through the small living room into the even smaller kitchen. "What happened to my nearly full bottle of Black Bush?"

"Whether the bottle is nearly full or nearly empty depends on how you look at it."

"I can see that you've been doing more than looking at it."

"Damn straight. That bottle of Irish whisky, Carole Lombard, and I have pretty well determined the identity of the killer, or at least I've narrowed it down to a precious few."

"That's amazing, Sherlock," said McGovern, with a heavy overlay of facetiousness. "With only the dribs and drabs of information you've received regarding the crime scenes, most of it provided by myself, I might add, you've nailed the killer. Mind telling me how you managed to accomplish that feat?"

"You know I never reveal my methods, Watson. Not only that, but I'm certain this villain wears a mask, Watson. A familiar mask, even a friendly one. The good news is, that even with this Agatha Christie–like cornucopia of dead bodies lying all around us, our dedicated little perpetrator's work is not yet complete. The only way to prove the identity of our little problem child, Watson, is to catch the fiend red-handed. Do you follow me, Watson?"

"I can't follow you, the way you're pacing back and forth. There'd be no room to turn around. We'd bump into each other."

"Good point, Watson. Your rapierlike grasp of a situation at hand always ceases to amaze me."

"What do we do now, Sherlock?"

"We finish the Black Bush, Watson."

"I'll get out the magnifying glasses."

There are conventional ways of solving life's little problems, and then there are unconventional ways. Crime-solving is no different. You can paint by the numbers, you can color between the lines, you can borrow somebody's notes for Abnormal Psychology 101. You can join the police academy, you can become a federal agent and wear a certain kind of sunglasses, you can follow all the rules, connect all the dots, and finally, you'll get to a place where you never question authority because you are the authority. In the matter at hand I did not have the luxury of employing any of this esteemed methodology. All I could do, in fact, was frisbee my soul into hell in the hope some three-headed, flatulent dog might catch it.

THIRTY

O ne definite advantage of having a very small circle of friends
is that it lessens the possibility that one of them might be a
serial killer. Nonetheless, these days, who can be completely
sure? During the height of my Peruvian marching powder days, I
performed regularly on Sunday nights at the Lone Star Café. The
place was architected in such a weird way that only the downstairs
bartender had an unobscured view of the stage, but everybody could
see every patron as they came through the revolving doors and
moved gingerly past the narrow catwalk between the bar and the
stage. Many strange people came through those doors those nights,
strangers to me, strangers possibly to themselves, resembling Latin
American drug kingpins and mild-mannered shoe salesmen with
dark sides of their lives bigger than Dallas. Sometimes, when a really
wiggy stranger came in, I would cry out from the microphone in a
frightening falsetto like a deranged mynah bird, "I know your
secret!" This always got a laugh from the crowd, but was also danger-
ous because, especially in those drug-addled, highly paranoid times,
just about everybody did have a secret and some of them were
darker, indeed, than the dark side of the moon, or a marriage, or a

garbage truck. I, alone, did not have a secret. That's because, to paraphrase Ted Mann, the only secrets I kept were the ones I'd forgotten.

I spent only a few days hiding out at McGovern's but, because of McGovern, and the small size of the apartment, it felt more like the tedious, interminable time frame of the Peloponnesian Wars. To be totally fair to McGovern, he was providing me with what little news I could obtain regarding the murder spree, which relegated me pretty much to the situation of the blind man and the elephant. Added to that, I also knew, like everybody else, what I read in the papers. Unfortunately, most of what I had read was written by McGovern. This is not to say that McGovern wasn't a good, even a great, journalist; it's just never really best foot forward for the fountainhead of all knowledge to be derived from a large Irishman who once combed his hair before meeting a racehorse.

I had my own ideas, of course, as to the identity of the killer, but I still had to rule out what was impossible, thereby leaving me only with what was possible, thereby removing all questions and doubt and leaving only a fine residue of ennui and unpleasantness. I began by running up McGovern's phone bill, calling everyone and anyone I knew who might be capable of saying, "More eggnog?" This included Washington Ratso, who had an alibi because he lived and worked in Washington, Will Hoover, who had an alibi because he lived and worked in Hawaii, Kent Perkins, Dr. Jim Bone, Roscoe West, Billy Swan, the aforementioned Ted Mann, John Mankiewicz, Dylan Ferrero, Dwight Yoakam, Bob Dylan, Hitler, Jesus Christ, and Butch Huff from Ashland, Kentucky. They all knew me well but they hadn't the means to have created a necklace of necrology in New York. To borrow a tiresome sports analogy, I was touching all bases. Some of the bases became slightly incredulous and mildly irritated when they began to discern the true purpose of my call, but when you're an amateur private investigator on the run from the cops, that comes with the territory.

Then I got down to dealing with that small, finite universe of people who did have the means, those who lived and worked, or shirked, in New York. Like I said, mine was an asymmetrical campaign, performed without the massive data, manpower, or authority at the beck and call of the NYPD. More than ever I was relying on cowboy logic, native sensitivity, androgynous intuition, hints, suspicions, gut feelings, personal experience, and other, more spiritually abstract whims and pet peeves that, no doubt, neither Sherlock nor Nero Wolfe would have countenanced. Some would point out, of course, that both of those great men were fictional characters. To this, I would respond that the world of fiction and the world of nonfiction are overlapping worlds in which much of what comprises the nonfiction world may not be true, and much of what makes up the world of fiction may, indeed, be true if the reader knows how to read between the lines. Hopefully, there will be more than one reader. And so it was that I navigated between these worlds in much the way I'd done for most of my life, ever aware of the little-known fact that many centuries ago Tahitian sailors were believed to have made their way to the Hawaiian Islands in rudimentary canoes, and these noble, primitive men, as they crossed thousands of miles of uncharted, often starless seas, in order to detect ever-so-subtle ocean currents, were said to have, on occasion, placed their scrotums on the wooden floors of their canoes for navigational purposes.

Calling the Village Irregulars and other close friends was a whole other help line, of course. It was hard to see any of them doing the evil deeds, but I didn't want to wind up like the nice old neighbor lady who lived next door to Charles Whitman, who climbed the Texas Tower in 1967 and shot to death sixteen people. I didn't want to be interviewed by local TV only to say, "He was such a nice boy." The truth is they never are. Nice boys can turn evil on a rusty dime. Friends can stab you in the back. Women will betray you when you least expect it. To the cold eye of the private investigator, nothing is what it appears to be. Most people are like Ratso, living in an inno-cent Dr. Watson wonderland. When they visit somebody they haven't seen for some time, they always make some gushing remark such as, "I've never seen him happier in his life." Three days later the person always blows his brains out. Ironically, the closer we get to other peo-ple, the harder it often is to see behind the mask. Yet this killer seemed almost to be speaking to me, beseeching me, screaming my name.

I narrowed the universe, smaller and smaller. All the usual suspects lived in New York. All of them had the means except Rambam, who was out of the country for several of the murders. Or at least he claimed he was. He was due back soon and I, of course, would have to check him out on his alibi, which was not going to make for a pleas-ant welcome home. Even McGovern and Ratso could not be over-looked. Hell, nobody could be overlooked until this killer was caught. So I went deeper into McGovern's liquor cabinet, found a bottle of Old Grandad this time, and began making some exploratory calls.

I won't bore you with the blow-by-blow details, the people who took it personally, the ones who said I belonged in a mental institu-tion, or the methods I employed with which to extract from them the information I needed. Some, like Brennan, were downright hostile and uncooperative. Some, like Chinga, never responded to my calls at all. Few of the Irregulars, of course, had the motivation to commit these heinous acts. Few of them, indeed, had any motivation at all. The ones who did, seemed to evince little enthusiasm for my investi-gation. Winnie was more interested in discussing the new dance classes she was organizing. Pete Myers was consumed with his upcoming one-man motorcycle odyssey in Mexico. Besides, the blower was far from the best tool for unearthing the truth about human beings. I cradled the blower at last, sat down on the oceango-ing couch, and poured a very large, adult portion of Old Grandad into an appropriately stemmed glass. I was just preparing to pour a hefty shot down my neck, when the aforementioned blower began ringing. I killed the shot, then collared the instrument. First things first.

"Start talkin'," I said, in an Old Grandad–strangled voice I hardly recognized. Evidently, the caller didn't either.

"Kinky?" asked the rather dubious female.

"Yeah, it's me. Something just went down the wrong way. Who's this?"

"Heather Lay," she purred.

Something about the lazy, sleepy way she pronounced her name excited me. I'd been working the case pro bono, but the sound of her voice gave new meaning to the term.

"I got this number from your friend Ratso," she said. "Or should I say Larry. When I called the number on your card and left a message and didn't hear from you, I got worried. So I looked up Larry Sloman in the phonebook and we had a long chat. You are being careful, aren't you?"

"I'm wearing my rubbers," I said.

There was something about Heather that made me want to go on listening to her forever. I hardly knew this person, I thought, yet it felt like I'd known her all my life. She didn't behave like any other woman I'd ever met. And she didn't seem to be wearing a mask.

"Look, Kinky. Funny to call you Kinky. I hope you catch whoever it was who killed Jordan, but more important, I want you to be safe. I have to admit that Jordan's death has liberated me, and I think that all started when you visited me the other day. I knew right away that you weren't really a friend of Jordan's. You couldn't have been. You're too sweet."

I'm not often afflicted with the condition of being at a loss for words. On this occasion, however, I could think of absolutely nothing to say. I felt deeply moved. I felt exhilarated and hopeful. I felt, well, liberated.

"Not as sweet as you," I finally managed to mutter.

"You don't know that yet," she said. "What're you going to do now?"

"I can't hide from life and the cops forever. I'll take you out to dinner for a big hairy steak."

"I'm a vegetarian."

"I'm a vagitarian."

"Good," she said with a shy chuckle. "We're both on healthy diets."

"The first thing I've got to do, though, is to go back to my loft and change clothes."

"I thought it was staked out?"

"Is there anything Ratso *didn't* tell you?"

"He didn't tell me you have brown eyes that twinkle. I saw that for myself. But won't you be arrested if you go back?"

"I don't think so. We just might have to put up with a few chaperones on our first date."

"How romantic."

"You see, the cops don't really want me, Heather. They just want to know what I know."

"And what *do* you know?"

"I know who killed Jordan," I said.

THIRTY-ONE

John Lennon once remarked, "Life is what happens when you're making plans." John didn't mention it, but death is also what sometimes happens when you're finally becoming interested in your social calendar. The killer struck again before I was even able to leave McGovern's. An operational pattern that moved this quickly might not have been surprising to veteran serial case profilers, but, I must report, the eighth killing caused me to quickly kill what was left of the Old Grandad. Each man kills the thing he loves. Oscar Wilde.

News of the eighth murder came to me first from McGovern and then from Ratso, the latter individual needlessly stating that he could not reveal his "sauces." Not that anyone cared to know. No details were vouchsafed yet, the NYPD obviously circling the paddy wagons on this one. The crush of high-profile media pressure was blotting out what little sun there was in New York. "All the press has gone apeshit," Ratso had shouted over the blower. "It's bigger than Son of Sam, Kinkstah!" McGovern did provide one small detail of the crime, for whatever it was worth. The victim this time was an older man, apparently. Quite a bit older than the other victims. What that meant was anybody's guess.

It was time, I figured, to roll the dice. If, indeed, I was correct in my suspicions, I might as well find out before the perpetrator got up to twelve maids a'milking. I knew I was going to get one chance and only one chance at this, so I had to be right the first time. And not only did I have to be right, I had to prove my case to the cops and, perhaps more important, to my own satisfaction. But you've got to break an egg if you want *huevos rancheros*. Sometimes, you've got to break two.

I glanced out McGovern's window into the little alley behind his building. The weather was dark and foreboding, with periodic lightning forking the bleak skyline. Rain or shine, I thought, pretty damn soon I had to deliver the mail. There's a dark and a troubled side of life, the old song goes. There's a bright and a sunny side, too. As we live in this war-torn, weatherbeaten world, it seems to get harder every day to keep on the sunny side. A vision I held in my heart of Heather was helping to boost my spirits for what I suspected was coming to a theater near me soon. It was clearly time to leave the nest. Besides, I'd been out of Cuban cigars for several days now, a situation that always seemed to radically alter my personality. But how would anyone know?

I wrote McGovern a brief note late that afternoon, thanking him for his horsepitality. Gray walls of rain were beginning to slant down at strange, unnatural angles outside McGovern's window. It was the kind of weather with which Sherlock himself might've felt quite at home. I knew I wasn't really Sherlock. Under my current operating circumstances, it was going to be impossible to totally rule out the impossible. Sometimes, aboard this ship of fools, you just have to settle for a sailor's luck.

I borrowed an old overcoat of McGovern's that I doubted he'd miss. It was bigger than a circus tent, but not quite as garish. The evening was getting colder and darker, almost, it seemed, by force of habit, but the rain had slacked off enough to create the kind of visibility required for a small child to land a paper airplane. An investigation is a lot like life, I thought as I walked, and the really important little pieces of any mystery are quite often the ones that have been there all the time. If you miss them in the beginning, you're very likely to wind up lost at the end. And sometimes it's all very simple, really. Sometimes a cigar is just a cigar. I don't mean to be too cryptic here, but if I told you how I know what I know, you'd say, "Hell, everybody knows that!" which, of course, everybody doesn't. That's why, over the years, I've made it a practice not to reveal either my methods or myself in public.

I walked down Jane in the rain. I walked down Fourth Street past Twelfth and Bank and Perry to Seventh Avenue. I walked up Vandam glancing casually around for signs of surveillance, seeing none in evidence. Something told me they were there, however. Kind of like when you know a Peeping Tom is watching you. If the tech guy Anderson, whom Cooperman had brought in as a substitute for Fox, had bugged the loft, as I suspected, the street surveillance would be lying very low. By the time I got near 199B Vandam I was cold and wet and numb and I didn't really give a damn if anyone was watching from the street or from the sky. Like a man in a trance, I looked down and saw a shivering black-and-white bundle lying at the foot of the door to the building. Two familiar green eyes looked up at me. I picked her up and held her to my chest like a tramp on the street clinging to an angel.

"My God!" I said. "Where have you been?"

The cat, of course, said nothing.

THIRTY-TWO

Cats walk the miles and the years with the graceful resilience people can only dream of. Whether out of loyalty, love, or whether, like us, they are also creatures of narrow habit, they often do manage to come back just in the nick of time. Their adventures, their journeys, remain in their eyes and in our imaginations. The trail of a cat, like the trail of a killer, is shielded from the world and shrouded by the smoke of life and the fog of death. Where have you been, my charming young one?

Once I'd gotten her back up in the loft I noticed that she really didn't seem much the worse for wear after all these many months. She looked a little thin, but so had Jesus. In the back of a cabinet, the cat food was still there. I hadn't had the heart to throw it away. Or maybe it was personal sloth. She ate a can of tuna like it was a last supper. I'm not contending there was necessarily a piece of Jesus in that cat. I'm only saying that if you look into the eyes of a stray animal, you can sometimes find the sanctuary of the god of your choosing. If you can make room in your heart to give that animal sanctuary, you truly have opened the gates of heaven a little bit wider.

So now everything was falling into place. The cat was home, resting on my desk under her heat lamp. The investigation was reaching its end game. If Cooperman had his person of interest, I had mine as well. And with the pleasant aspect of a candlelit dinner with Heather in the near future, it was almost enough to make me believe in astrology. Who needed big hairy steaks when your destiny was written in the stars?

"It's just like old times," I said to the cat, as I lifted Sherlock's cap and plucked out a fresh Cuban cigar from deep within his gray matter department. It might have been some kind of anthropomorphic bullshit, but I'd have sworn the cat was smiling.

"This conversation may have to be a little guarded," I said, as I lopped off the butt of the Montecristo Number 2, the same kind of cigar that had figured in the rather unsavory death of one Ron Lucas. "It's possible that what we're saying may be recorded for all posterity."

The cat did not care a flea about posterity; the only thing she cared about at that moment was that her own posterior was warm and dry. Perhaps you think this rather a short-sighted, selfish outlook to have. If that's what you think, you don't know cats. And you don't know people. You might make a good morally rigid, well-meaning Dr. Watson, but you'd never have what it takes to become a lonely, truth-seeking missile like Sherlock Holmes.

"Listen to that!" I ejaculated, as I fired up the cigar, which is hard to do by any man's standard. "If I'm not mistaken, it's a blessing from above!"

And so it was. For the first time in many months, the familiar footnotes of the lesbian dance class were pounding with dull, syncopated thuds on the floor above, which, in weaker moments, I liked to refer to as my ceiling. Not only was this a welcome break in the somber silence that had for so long enveloped the loft, but also, I figured, it would create a perfect nightmare for anyone who happened to be eavesdropping with a listening device.

"It makes you wonder," I commented to the cat, "if God might really be a woman."

The cat didn't much approve of this kind of talk. The cat was a free-form fundamentalist who'd once been a Baptist until she realized they didn't hold 'em under long enough. I didn't think any less of the cat because she was a fundamentalist. Everybody's a fundamentalist about the things that really matter to them. That's one of the built-in little tragedies of the human race.

"I'll let you in on a little secret," I confided to the cat, as I poured a long, medicinal shot of Jameson's into the old bull's horn. "I have two persons of interest in my life at the moment. One is a particularly fiendish, psychotic mass killer. The other, newly liberated from years of abuse, is a young woman I've only just met. I plan to see both of them tomorrow night. My dance card, as you can imagine, is rather full."

The cat took in this information with no small measure of incredulity. A cat usually doesn't believe anything until she reads it in *The New York Times.*

"I'll have to call Heather first, of course. She could be the future ex–Mrs. Kinky Friedman. That's Heather, rhymes with feather. You can relate to that, can't you?"

Unfortunately, the cat was asleep by this time. I was busy pouring my second bolt of Jameson's down my neck. Things seemed almost back to normal. I picked up the blower on the left and called Heather and we exchanged a few pleasantries. I told her I had a little private investigator business tomorrow night, but I'd call her afterward and maybe we could have a late dinner.

"Please be careful," she said, in that intimate, husky-sounding voice I was quickly becoming accustomed to. It just seemed to go with coffee in bed. Or skip the coffee.

"'Please be careful's' my middle name," I said. "It's a longish middle name. Been hell on monograms. But don't worry, I will."

I was perhaps being a bit flippant with someone who'd just lost somebody close to her, but maybe flippant was all I had in stock that night. After all, it'd been a long time since anybody'd wanted me to please be careful.

"I hope I'm not being nosy," she said, "but have you worked things out with the police?"

"Not really."

"Then you're taking Ratso with you on your little private investigator business tomorrow night?"

"Not really. There are some things you just have to do by yourself. My mother once told me that when I was a baby and she tried to feed me, I would say 'Shelf! Shelf!' That meant I wanted to do it myself."

"You must have been a beautiful baby. But don't you think it's time you learned to do it with somebody else?"

"It's past time," I said, and I meant it. "But, Heather, there is a certain kind of person with a dark, ugly secret that's been festering down deep inside them, maybe for most of their life. That kind of person is dying to unburden himself, but also killing to keep himself from having to do so. There's no logic to it. It doesn't make sense to a rational mind. But if you're the right person to talk to, and you approach this individual at the right place and the right time, they just might cop to it. One thing's for sure. In a million years, they'll never share it with the rest of the class."

"I understand," she said. And maybe she did.

I told her again that I'd call her when I got through. I'd already told her too much, but I could see that it wasn't enough. There are things you'd love to tell people you love, but you never seem to tell them. You just trust that they've always known.

THIRTY-THREE

That night, with the cat curled up next to me, I dreamed of Lottie. When Lottie Cotton was born on September 6, 1902, in the tiny southeast Texas town of Liberty, there were no airplanes in the sky. There were no SUVs, no superhighways, no cell phones, no televisions. When Lottie was laid to rest this past July in Houston, there was a black Jesus looking after her from the wall of the funeral chapel. Most biblical scholars agree today that Jesus, being of North African descent, very likely may have been black. But Lottie was always spiritually color-blind; her Jesus was the color of love. She spent her entire life looking after others. One of them, I'm privileged to say, was me.

Lottie was not a maid. She was not a nanny. She did not live with us. We were not rich rug rats raised in River Oaks. We lived in a middle-class neighborhood of Houston. (My mother was one of the first speech therapists hired by the Houston Independent School District; my father traveled throughout the Southwest doing community relations work.) Lottie helped cook and babysit during the day and soon became part of our family. I was old enough to realize, yet young enough to know, that I was in the presence of a special person. Laura Bush, my occasional pen pal, had this to say about Lottie in a recent letter, and I don't think she'd mind my sharing it with you: "Only special ladies earn the title of 'second mother.' She must have been a remarkable person, and I know you miss her."

There are not many people like Lottie left in this world. Few of us, indeed, have the time and the love to spend our days and nights looking after others. Most of us take our responsibilities to our own families seriously. Many of us work hard at our jobs. Some of us even do unto others as we would have them do unto us. But how many would freely, willingly, lovingly share the architecture of the heart with two young boys and a young girl, a cocker spaniel named Rex, and a white mouse named Archimedes?

One way or another for almost fifty-five years, wherever I traveled in the world, Lottie and I managed to stay in touch. I now calculate that when Lottie sent me birthday cards in Borneo when I was in the Peace Corps, she was in her early sixties, an age that I myself am now rapidly, if disbelievingly, approaching. She also remained in touch with my brother, Roger, who lives in Maryland, and my sister, Marcie, who lives in Vietnam. To live a hundred years on this troubled planet is a rare feat. But to maintain contact with your "children" for all that length of time, and for them to have become your dear friends in later years, is rarer still.

For Lottie did not survive one century in merely the clinical sense; she was as sharp as a tack until the end of her days. At the ripe young age of ninety-nine, she could sit at the kitchen table and knowledgeably discuss politics or religion—or stuffed animals. Lottie left behind an entire menagerie of teddy bears and other stuffed animals, each of them with a name and personality all its own. She also left behind two live animals, dogs named Minnie and Little Dog, who had followed her and protected her everywhere she went. (Minnie is a little dog named for my mother, and Little Dog, as might be expected, is a big dog.)

Lottie is survived by her daughter, Ada Beverly (the two of them have referred to each other as "Mama" for at least the past thirty years), and one grandson, Jeffery. She's also survived by Roger, Marcie, and me, who live scattered about a modern-day world, a world that has gained so much in technology yet seems to have lost those sacred recipes for popcorn balls and chocolate-chip cookies. "She was a seasoned saint," a young preacher who'd never met her said at her funeral. But was it too late, I wondered, to bless the hands that prepared the food? And there were so many other talents in Lottie's gentle hands, not the least of which was the skill to be a true mender of the human spirit.

I don't know what else you can say about someone who has been in your life forever, someone who was always there for you, even when "there" was very far away. Lottie was my mother's friend, she was my friend, and now she has a friend in Jesus. She always had a friend in Jesus, come to think of it. The foundation of her faith was as strong as the foundation of the railroad tracks she helped lay as a young girl in Liberty. Lottie, you've outlived your very bones, darling. Yours is not the narrow immortality craved by the authors, actors, and artists of this world. Yours is the immortality of a precious passenger on the train to glory, which has taken you from the cross-ties on the railroad to the stars in the sky.

By day and by night, each in their turn, the sun and the moon gaze through the window, now and again reflecting upon the gold-and-silver pathways of childhood. The pathways are still there, but we cannot see them with our eyes. Nor shall we ever again tread lightly upon them with our feet. Yet as children, we never suspect we might someday lose our way. We think we have all the time in the world.

I am still here, Lottie. And Ada gave me two of the teddy bears that I sent you long ago. As I write these words, they sit on the windowsill looking after me. Some might say they are only stuffed animals. But, Lottie, you and I know what's really inside them. It's the stuff of dreams.

THIRTY-FOUR

The first thing I did the next morning, after feeding the cat, and preparing the espresso machine for launch, was to call Ratso. His voice was a little grating when it happened to be your first human contact of the day, but this time I really needed his help. For one thing, I didn't want to risk leaving the loft unless it was on fire. For another, Ratso had something I wanted.

"Kinkstah!" he shouted through the blower. "Heather seems to like the Kinkstah!"

"She seems like a nice person."

"What do you mean, 'She seems like a nice person'?" Ratso rattled on like a subway train. "She's hot, baby! She's hot!"

"Well, it was very nice of you to play the little Jewish match-maker—"

"Anytime, Kinkstah! Anytime! But I hope you're not straying too far from the investigation. I mean, a little R&R is fine, but according to my count we've now got eight vics and no perps! What're we planning to do about that, Sherlock?"

"I'm planning to meet with the perp tonight."

"Great! When and where?"

"Up to the perp."

"Just let me know, Sherlock, and I'll be there."

"That won't be necessary, Watson. Tonight's encounter with the perp, for many reasons, of necessity, must be Sirhan-Sirhan-party-of-one."

"Wait a minute, Sherlock! I've been with you every step of the way! I've done all the legwork with you! Now you're going to solve the case alone? What happened to your deep, latent homosexual attachment to your fucking wonderful, loyal Dr. Watson? What happened to my being the fixed point in a changing age?"

"There is a fixed point on top of your head, Watson."

"I can't believe you'd lead Watson to water and not let him drink. I can't believe you'd show Watson the promised land and not let him go there."

"Pinch yourself, Watson, this is all very unbecoming of you. Surely you know that a perp confesses to the good cop only after the bad cop has left the room. Surely you know that while some may preach to the choir, none *confess* to the choir. Surely you know that when a sinner confesses to a priest, it's always one on one."

"Surely you know that when a priest bullfucks his best friend, then tells the pope he thought he was an altar boy—"

"Watson, this is all very unbecoming of you."

Treat children like adults and adults like children, my father had always said. Ratso, indeed, had a temperament quite similar to that of a small child, or a playful puppy. He was passionate in his beliefs, but he was also quite easily distracted. I utilized my father's dictum with him now.

"There is one matter, Watson, of the utmost importance, that you and you alone are uniquely equipped to deal with. As you well know, for reasons other than malaria this time, I am a virtual prisoner of Vandam Street. I leave the loft only at great personal risk. But there is an object, Watson, that is currently in your possession, Watson, that I must have, Watson!"

"Sure, Sherlock. What is it?"

"That porn video."

I could hear the wheels turning in Ratso's head. I could feel his mind moving to a different track. I took the opportunity to strike a kitchen match on my jeans and resurrect a dead Cuban soldier.

"All right, Kinkstah! She seems like a nice person, Kinkstah! Maybe she's naughty and nice, Kinkstah! Maybe she likes big, mean cowboys! Maybe you'll throw on the porn tape and then ride her hard and put her up wet, Kinkstah!"

"Ah, Watson, your mind, my friend, is so facile and intuitive! Is there any aspect of any relationship that can evade your prying, prurient gaze?"

"I guess not, Sherlock," said Ratso, with a sadly misguided measure of pride. "I'll drop it by later this morning."

"Good work, Watson! Of those to whom much has been given, much is expected."

True to his word, Ratso dropped the porn video off later that morning. As the lesbian dance class had temporarily fallen silent, I encouraged him to speak in guarded tones. It was a challenge for him to whisper.

"Heather's going to love this!" he said. "Give her a few shots from the ol' bull's horn as a leg-opener, then put the video on and you'll probably ram the ol' avenger home on the first date!"

"Ah, Watson, even in this jaded Victorian age, it's comforting to know that chivalry is not dead."

After Ratso had taken his leave, I made one more call. Without entirely tipping my hand, I revealed a few cards. They were enough to set up a rendezvous for later that night.

THIRTY-FIVE

I was feeding the cat some tuna and feeding myself a leftover bagel when the phones rang. It was the middle of the afternoon and things were pretty quiet; the lesbian dance class, apparently, having gone into remission. I walked over to the desk with a lit cigar in my mouth, a cup of hot coffee in one hand, and a lukewarm bagel in the other, and tried to pick up the phone. It was one of the more difficult things I've attempted to do in my life and it was not entirely met with success. As I sat down in the chair, a dollop of very hot coffee splashed onto my crotch, the receiver dropped to the floor, and my cigar fell into my half-full cup of coffee. I cursed loudly enough for the cat to stop eating her tuna and to jump onto the desk and shamelessly rubberneck for some moments. I reached to pick up the blower from off the floor, breathing hard and still cursing under my breath. Then the chair fell over.

"Start talkin'," I said gruffly, once I'd righted myself.

"If I knew you were going to be this excited to hear from me," said Rambam, "I never would've left. What the hell's going on? A terrorist attack in the West Village? The Tourette Syndrome Olympics? A do-it-yourself hemorrectomy?"

"All of the above. Welcome back."

"Was *that* the lesbian dance class?"

"No. I think they've taken five."

"Five what? It sounded like the circus got to town just about the time the sky was falling."

"No, it's nothing. I'm just a little jumpy I guess."

"What's there to be jumpy about? Just because a psycho's croaked eight scumbags and the cops think you did it? Nothin' to be jumpy about. Hell, if it was me, I'd jump on the next plane back to Angkor Wat."

"Wat? Can't hear you. I've got a lesbian dance class in my ear."

To tell the truth, everything was pretty quiet now. No lesbian dance class. No terrorists. Just waiting for the anointed hour when I would drop the axe.

"What *are* you doing about the investigation?" asked Rambam pointedly. "Of course if the murder spree goes on much longer it might develop into a rather effective method of dealing with sex abuse. Not to mention population control."

"Oh, the investigation. I think I've solved it. I'm meeting with my own person of interest at an undisclosed location tonight."

"What undisclosed location?" shouted Rambam. "You mean you've got no backup? Other than Ratso, I mean."

"Ratso wasn't invited."

"Well, at least you'll have the cops."

"No cops. My person of interest is too cagey for that. Besides, if the cops are along I'll never get the goods."

"Surely they've had you under surveillance for some time. And your place is probably bugged as we speak. How do you plan to avoid them?"

"I'll use a trick an old friend of mine named Steve Rambam once told me about. It involves an X-rated video on loan from the Ratso Collection."

"Fucking great. Suppose you're one on one with your person of interest and he *does* turn out to be the killer? Then what do you do? Call 911?"

"Can't say more. Little ears may be listening."

"Okay. It's your funeral."

After I'd cradled the blower with Rambam, I typed up some notes for a while, fed the cat some more tuna, and then the two of us took a peaceful power nap together on the davenport by the front fire escape. By the time we leapt sideways it was eight o'clock and dark outside. I took an espresso over to the window and looked down at Vandam Street. There seemed to be a lot of activity tonight and the sleeping garbage trucks tended to obscure some of the view, so it was hard to pick out any signs of surveillance. The cops were probably there, all right. In a strange way I suppose you could say we were both looking out for each other.

The cat jumped up on the windowsill and looked out into the dark, cold night. She was watching the place we call New York. An old lady moving ever-so-slowly with her aluminum Jerry Jeff Walker. A wino that looked like Walt Whitman whizzing on a wall. A young woman trying vainly to hail a cab, her hand held high like the Statue of Liberty. Lots of traffic going by. Lots of pedestrians moving like chess pieces from one square to another.

"So many people," I said to the cat. "So few comets."

I put Ratso's porn tape on the machine and turned up the volume. Just in case anybody was listening, they'd hear sounds of heated lovemaking, indicating I'd gotten lucky and would be in for the evening. At about eight-thirty I put on McGovern's old overcoat, grabbed three cigars from Sherlock's head, and walked to the door.

I left the cat in charge.

TRANSCRIPT OF INTERVIEW
WITH STEVEN RAMBAM

Case # 2004—743 (Friedman, Kinky)
(Homicide, multiple)

MC= Mort Cooperman

SR = Steve Rambam

MC: This is February 2, 200_. I'm Detective Sergeant Mort Cooperman of the New York Police Department. I'm continuing the interview with Steve Rambam, a white male, forty-two years old. Place of residence (refused). Place of employment (refused). Also present is Detective Sergeant Buddy Fox. Mr. Rambam is aware that this interview is being recorded.

MC: Okay, Rambam. So how'd you know what time the subject would be leaving his loft?

SR: I didn't. I staked the place out just like your guys. When he exited through a back alley I tailed him, just like your guys didn't.

MC: Why am I not surprised? Where'd the subject go?

SR: Walked two blocks to Hudson. Got into a cab.

MC: All right. And you followed the cab?

SR: No. I followed a large double-decker sight-seeing bus.

MC: Don't get smart with me, Rambam. Where'd the cab take the subject?

SR: Kinky got out of the cab at the Brooklyn Bridge.

MC: The Brooklyn Bridge.

SR: You know. The big steel thing they built across the river?

MC: I'm warning you, Rambam. What happened next?

SR: He paid the cab and started heading up the pedestrian walk onto the bridge.

MC: What'd you do?

SR: It was pretty dark. So I pulled the car over and got out my night vision scope. There was no activity on the pedestrian walk so it was pretty easy for me to keep sight of him.

MC: What'd you do next?

SR: The further he went up the bridge, the more nervous I got. I thought for sure the cops would be monitoring him. I got out of the car and looked around. No cops. Nobody.

MC: Okay. Then what?

SR: I followed him on foot. I kept a good distance between us, stayed behind the girders as much as possible.

MC: You took the night vision scope with you?

SR: Yes. From behind the girders I could see him clearly.

MC: Did you see anyone else on the pedestrian walk?

SR: Yes. There was somebody waiting at the middle of the bridge.

MC: Did you recognize that person.

SR: Yes.

MC: Who was that person?

SR: Winnie Katz.

MC: What did you think when you saw her there?

SR: I thought she was a long way from her lesbian dance class.

MC: Were you surprised?

SR: At first, yes. Then I thought about it for a second and it all made sense.

MC: What made sense?

SR: She's the one who supposedly found the dead guy's wallet in Kinky's loft. She could've just as easily placed it there herself. Also, the victims were all scumbags whose hobby was abusing women. It fit perfectly. I later learned that the eighth victim, the old geezer, was her child-molesting, dirtbag stepfather, who no doubt played a large hand in getting her started on the wrong track.

MC: Save the psychology. Okay. You're on the bridge now. What'd you see?

SR: Kinky walked up to the middle of the bridge.

MC: And?

SR: They started talking.

MC: How close were you to them?

SR: Maybe halfway from the base of the bridge to where they were standing.

MC: You could see them but they couldn't see you?

SR: Right. I was behind a girder with the night scope.

MC: What happened then?

SR: They talked. She seemed to be very distraught. Kinky appeared to be trying to talk her down from the bridge.

MC: Go on.

SR: It seemed to be working. She seemed to become more relaxed. Kinky was holding a hand out to her. She was slowly moving toward him.

MC: Go on.

SR: Then she suddenly broke and lunged for the side. Kinky tried to grab her. They struggled.

MC: What did you do?

SR: I ran toward them as fast as I could. As I ran, I saw them both go over the side.

MC: What did you do then?

SR: Well, I didn't jump in after them. I called 911. Asked for the Harbor Patrol.

MC: Yes. We have transcripts of that 911 call. What'd you do then?

SR: What the hell do you think I did? I cursed the goddamn cops for letting the whole thing spin out of control like this. It was *your* fucking investigation, not Kinky's. By this time, you should've been right on top of *both* of them. If the cops had been doing their job, this never would've happened. Where the hell *were* you? Why weren't you monitoring them? What were you doing? Investigating the Dunkin' Donuts Crime Family?

MC: Look, I know you're upset. I don't really blame you. Is there anything else? Any questions?

SR: Just one. I've always wondered about this. Which one of you two guys is Beavis?

Two Die in Suicide Pact
by Jayson Blair

Larry "Kinky" Friedman, a rapper from Receda, California, and Winnie Katz, who ran a day-care center in Queens, died last night in a fall from the Triboro Bridge. Mr. Friedman, best known for his recent hit, "Ol' Bill Lucas Had a Lotta Mucus," had been currently working on his autobiography with this writer. His friends remember him as a quiet, well-mannered, impeccably attired, pipe-smoking opera buff. Though Mr. Friedman's musical tastes included rap and opera, he was a man of many other pursuits, passions, and hobbies.

"He collected matchbooks from many restaurants," said his close friend Dr. Stephen Rambam, of the Midtown Ophthalmology Clinic. "He never missed a Yankee game," said Larry "Ratso" Sloman, a large, somewhat inebriated Irishman, "or was it the Mets?" "I'm sure he's now wandering in the raw poetry of time," said Mike McGovern, a priest at Our Lady of the Tire Iron.

Ms. Katz apparently met Mr. Friedman through an Internet chat room for Jewish singles. Their relationship, according to Chinga "Chonga" Chavin, a ventriloquist friend of Ms. Katz's, was loving, but could be stormy at times. "That's because she was a Mets fan," said Chavin. "Or was it the Yankees?" The autobiography upon which Mr. Friedman and I had been diligently working will now be published posthumously. The book contains stories about Mr. Friedman and his close friends, Willie Nelson and George W. Bush. Mr. Friedman had titled his book *My Willie, Your Bush*.

Though divers have searched the river, the bodies of the two star-crossed lovers have not been found.

This brings to 12,984 the number of suicides this year in the city. Police Captain Buddy Cooperman believes it's mostly due to overcrowding. "There are, of course," he says, "other factors." Ms. Katz has no next of kin. Mr. Friedman's family could not be located in Receda, California. He leaves behind only a stray cat who apparently had wandered into his loft.